Savage Vengeance!

Bacon City's rough, tough settlers knew that the Apache never struck at night—until one midnight five arrows, mark of Victorio, great Indian chief, tore deep into a white man's flesh.

Only the Sacaton Kid had a hunch that the bow was drawn by a white traitor's hand. But before he could prove it, Victorio's son was strung high on a treetop and the Apache cried for vengeance. War stained the Big Dry canyon red before the renegade was trapped and peace restored to the Territory.

This is action-packed drama of the hard-won, violent Southwest in the days before the Apache was tamed. "Fast-moving . . . colorful writing . . . absorbing plot."

—*The Chicago Tribune*

THE
BIG DRY

by

GEORGE GARLAND

WILDSIDE PRESS

To a courageous young man
TOMMY REED

CONTENTS

AUTHOR'S NOTE

BETWEEN the Gila and San Francisco Rivers in south-eastern New Mexico, the road drops suddenly off Cactus Flat in a maze of hairpin curves. Away to the east the mountains begin with a huge saddle hump that slopes to a horn, reminding one of a charging rhinoceros. It is the western jaw of a canyon's mouth. The long eastern jaw reaches farther out, sheer and colorful, seeming to stare back at the road like the patient eye of Time.

It is the Big Dry.

Who named it that nobody seems to know. A poet, perhaps, one with a healthy sense of reality, for the brutal opening stands there a monument to drought. It has seen water rushing down, melted snow from the peaks of the Mogollons, in a wasteful gift, unfriendly and mocking. It has witnessed the push of white men up to the fertile San Francisco Valley, to the gold mines, the return of ore-laden bullwagons, showers of arrows on covered wagons and stagecoaches, and the ambush of United States troopers by the Apache—and all on this road.

The picture, from the flat or "Soldiers' Hill," is the same now as in the day of the famous Apache chieftain Victorio, renegade or great warrior, but certainly a strategist, who fashioned a part of the true history of this land ahead of his pupil, Geronimo.

This setting, made to order for the Apache, seems next to perfect for an historical novel of the West. The writer takes the liberty of drawing upon his imagination in dealing with Victorio and his son-in-law, Terribio, and in weaving them into a purely fictional tale that ends under the forbidding gaze of the Big Dry.

1

THE SACATON KID

SILVER CITY lay miles behind the rider.

Young West rode at a shuffling gait relaxed to the motion of the saddle, apparently at peace with the world and himself. His eyes were glare-slitted as his gaze held fast to the southern heads of the Mogollon Mountains. Under the blistering afternoon sky the green of pines away in the distance seemed alive and dancing under shimmering heat waves.

He reined up and listened to a distant rumbling behind him. Knowing it was the stagecoach to Bacon and Queeny, he turned off the road into a bleached arroyo and waited behind a screen of scrub oak. If Cactus Williams sat in the driver's seat, this was the stage he had ridden north to intercept.

The tattoo of hoofs sounded closer. Soon the rolling wheels and crack of whip advised that the desert express was racing hard for Gila Crossing. It came on, tore on by in swirls of dust, clattering on, swaying, clinging to the twisting road like a train to a track. It followed a thin ribbon that was civilization's hard-won trail; it split a land where a house was a gamble, something chanced upon, where cattle calved in the Apaches' front yard. The mines up at Queeny drew it on. The lure was gold.

Of late many stories leaked down out of the valley and mountains. Victorio, chief of the Apaches, was recruiting among the tribes stationed on the reservation. Smokes columned upward, and the dry ground was scarred by travois, and squaws and children and sheep moved slowly in the Apache way out of Arizona Territory down to the White Rocks. The Fort Bayard command looked northeast, frowning at all it could not see.

However, if the rumor of the massacre up on Gutache Mesa were true, General Bent was probably bandoleering ammunition and alerting all outlying posts. Supposed to have happened at dawn four days back: two prospectors spread-eagled to the spokes of their wagon and killed by five burning arrows in each man. They were dead when Lieutenant Botts and his green troopers found them. Five arrows, five slashes in a horse's throat. Victorio was trying to convey something.

Young put it out of his mind. He was more interested in the item under the feet of Cactus Williams.

He rode on, holding his distance behind the old Concord until he heard its hip-and-hub splash in the Gila River. He then rowelled his pony and raced north, fording the river a good half-mile above the oncoming stage. Topping a small knoll by the road, he looked back, then rode down the side and dismounted. After tossing a gray hat into a clump of bear-grass, he placed a worn black hat on his head and pulled grimy tan trousers up over his dark ones. Next he tied a red bandana over his face.

The coach clattered nearer and a dust-devil started its spin in the road, raced west up the flats, and died in bantam fury. Young watched it, thinking there was a lot of dust to stir up out here. Had been, was, would be. In fact——

He had kicked up a dust-devil or two in his twenty-seven years. Noted as a pony express rider and scout, he had seen trouble in Arizona Territory, and up on the Platte during the Cheyenne campaign. But he knew the Apache better and, after an unsuccessful prospecting venture up in the Datil Mountains, he had again turned to scout for General Bent during the late Mescalero campaign. But he had not come off so well, due to friction between officers in the field, a Captain Corday and a hot-headed lieutenant named Dana. The latter, in disfavor now, blamed Young for the trap that took a dozen of his troopers. A scout's reward.

And now he was about to rob a stage.

The coach came on, and he watched the six-horse approach, a determined man who had no knowledge of the passengers inside. It would have mattered little if he had. He was of the breed, of one mind, a man of the dry country where dust and sun got under a man's skin and stirred up a brew that, like a poison, prolonged patience and whetted sensitiveness to a fine point.

The creaking or the stage was his signal. He got into the saddle and charged down from the blind side of the knoll. Cactus Williams saw him, reached for his rifle, dropped it when the horses snorted and reared. It was the advantage Young played for. The teams stood nervously still and Cactus reached high. Young slouched in the saddle, gun up, with deliberate ease. Not a word was spoken between them. Glances sufficed as Cactus studied the robber closely and found him more menacing by his unhurried manner.

The sack at Cactus's feet was handed over. Young motioned for the rifle, next, the pistol. Before the latter reached him, the coach door opened and five people stepped outside.

Quietly Young's thumb eased back the rifle hammer and the aim was set squarely on the crown of Cactus Williams' hat. The pistol leveled on the passengers.

All but one reached high. Only the girl stared fearlessly, curiously, a certain fascination making in her face. All of her registered in a flash on Young's mind. She had a pretty figure, and her eyes were green, decisive, and alive. She was looking at him with a controlled expression, like the shape of judgment withheld. Then it melted slowly, and a faint flush of color beat up under her skin.

One of the passengers darted a glance up at Cactus when Young appeared to relax. All of them knew the girl's eyes held him when his success and safety demanded that he look sharp. Then Young was taking them in one by one.

There was something familiar about the small man with determined gray eyes and red mustache. He knew who he was on second glance. Joe Sack, a man who had won his reputation on the right side of the law. But the girl was more interesting.

Cactus was looking for an advantage. He thought he saw it in Young's apparent carelessness and eased his hand down to his pistol. But Young had drawn his sight and now he saw the hand lift with the pistol. As both of them stared death in the face, Sack flipped up his coat in reach for his gun.

With the aim on Cactus fixed, Young had only to shift his pistol on Sack. Rifle and pistol spoke in unison. The bullet knocked the gun out of Sack's hand. The rifle slug tore through Cactus's hat crown, causing him to drop the pistol in a hurry.

The girl stared incredulously. When Young looked at her again, she seemed baffled. In her mind, despite rising anger and resentment, was something she could not help liking. Though a pair of eyes and sandy hair at the temples were all she saw above the bandana, she sensed the rest. And the bold careless attention he favored her with appealed to her as much as it angered her.

He was making a motion for the passengers to re-enter the stage. All obeyed except Sack and the girl. And she was about to raise a foot to the step when Young asked her name.

"Bonnie McQueen," she said sharply. "Who are you?"

"The Sacaton Kid," he replied. When she made no motion to get into the stage, he said, "Bonnie McQueen!" A cold light flickered across his eyes, then fell away into an amused expression. "Bonnie McQueen," he said again, as though the name meant something to him. He looked at the sack across his saddle.

9

On it was written what he already knew: A. T. McQUEEN, QUEENY MINE. McQueen, rich and powerful, was the big man of the 'Frisco Valley and the mining town. To Young West, he was something else.

"So you're McQueen's daughter," he said in a slow drawl that sounded like discovery. A light laugh sounded. "This is more than I anticipated, ma'am."

Her mouth had a pretty quirk to it and there was a singular attraction in her every movement. "Why don't you move on while you can?" she said, staring daggers at him.

Sack spoke up. "Maybe you'd like to hand over the payroll sack, young feller. We'll give you a good start."

There was a cogent quality in Sack's words. It emanated from his tone of voice and steady eyes and Young knew he was listening to a good proposition. There were a few men like Sack in the West. They stood firmly for law and order, fought for it. But the proposition wasn't for Young. He said so.

"Better listen to him," Bonnie said. "They'll bury the Sacaton Kid without bothering to ask who you really are."

"Now that could be, Bonnie," Young replied. "But aren't you thinking about your father's money?"

"He can spare all you took."

"Sure. And a lot more, I hear. But we don't want the big gun of the Valley robbed, do we? So just tell me where to return it."

"The A-T Ranch!" she said, not to be outdone by him. "Say around nine tomorrow night. We'll all be up waiting for you."

Her sarcasm tickled him. He chuckled and said, "I'll be seeing you, Bonnie."

He spurred his pony and raced off. Looking back, he saw Sack's hand fly up with a glint of metal in it. A shot and a close whine followed. But Young had seen more:

Bonnie's hand struck Sack's arm to deflect the aim.

Young rode north at a lazy gait, on past the stage stop and toward Cactus Flat, where night overtook him. A faint ghostly light etched the scenes about him, tipped the yucca and beargrass on the ridges like a memory of frost. A firebrand burned away up in the timber belt for an instant. He looked ahead and saw it repeated. Indian telegraph. The Apache was harmless at night.

The stars were low and heavy, and Bonnie's eyes continued to dig into his. Maybe the stars in his head were the ones he had seen burning brightly in her eyes. He had not expected her to stay with him all the way across Cactus Flat. But she

10

watched his every move as he dipped down to the serpentine curves of the road and stared across the dark expanse where the upthrust of rock marked the opening of Big Dry Canyon. Stopping his horse, he looked into the night and considered his future with unwelcome seriousness.

The heavens, the girl, or the canyon, or all combined, evoked in him an innate wisdom all his own and yet no part of him. He was balancing the things that made up his life—purpose and a finely calculated sense of vengeance—against what was anchored behind a woman's eyes. The ultimate goal was lost, tossed about in the ambivalence of his feelings, and he knew anger and resentment at the softer and finer instincts of his being.

He could not argue against purpose. What brought him out here was an unyielding thing. A woman's eyes could wait.

He nudged the horse with a foot and rode on north, up toward A. T. McQueen's country.

Bonnie knew somehow that she was working on the robber. She smiled up at the same stars he was seeing, urging him on with unspoken words. And like a woman she took a great delight in shaping his course even at a distance. She seemed to know that his fascinated look of the afternoon was still as fresh in his mind as in her memory. Some law of the universe made it so.

She ate supper at the stage stop, then climbed into the stage again. Cactus thought it best to travel at night. The news of the massacre of two prospectors up on Gutache Mesa influenced his decision. The Apache never struck at night.

As the coach rolled on and the other four passengers either slept or suffered the bumps in silence, Bonnie's mind wandered off aimlessly to her own life prior to this day; to her future. She looked back on her twenty-one years, seeing the West, cattle, horses, mines, and Indians. She had teethed on Indian talk. She rode a horse with easy grace. She played the organ, fashioned her own dresses and hats, ran the big McQueen house on the ranch as her mother had taught her to do before her death two years back, and even made decisions in the absence of her father and his manager, Luke Mason. She felt the full responsibility of the big A-T Ranch, enough to realize that she shouldn't have left it to go gallivanting down at Las Cruces for Lucy Summer's ball. But she had had fun. The Army officers danced divinely. She would not soon forget Captain Corday, or Lieutenant Dana, who was returning to Fort Mangus. In a way she was glad to be on the road home instead of waiting over for the ball at Fort Bayard tomorrow night. And Luke Mason would be glad also.

There! The thought of Luke brought her up sharply. She and Luke were engaged to be married, though no date had been set for a wedding. She looked thoughtfully out of the window at the stars winking on and off over the ragged edges of the Mogollons. In her mind, Luke was standing alongside Lieutenant Dana and a man whose full face she had never seen, the Sacaton Kid.

Luke was tall, suave, educated; from Denver. He knew finance and mining. The Sacaton Kid was a bandit. Dana, grim and sullen, was a soldier. Tame Luke loved comfort. The Kid, like Dana, probably slept outdoors, saddle for pillow. Luke took her for granted. His air was that of a man who, supposed to make a good marriage, had all but tied the knot. He drank and gambled in a quiet reserved manner that said, "Good policy to do so." What kind of game did the Kid play? Like he shot; like Dana fought?

Three men.

The green flashed behind her eyes. She would meet Luke Mason with a show of independence. Maybe she would exercise a catty streak and tell him how the Army officers slid across the dance floor with her as though they had moonlight in their veins.

She slept a little, opened her eyes, slept some more. As the night wore out, the stage reached the Mormon settlement where two passengers got off. The cowboy said he would ride ahead on the outrider's horse to Bacon with news of the robbery. This left her with only Sack for company. Both were wide awake when the stage rolled on. He asked about her father, saying he had known McQueen for years, that A. T. would be surprised to learn that he was the new deputy sheriff, among other things.

"Deputy sheriff!" Bonnie exclaimed. "Then you're duty bound to catch the Sacaton Kid."

"Right. And I'll do it." He added. "Somehow."

"Deputies don't last long in Bacon or Queeny," she reminded.

"So I've heard," came the soft-spoken reply.

"What did you mean when you said you were the new deputy, *among other things?*"

Sack thought he could answer her in two words, "Apache trouble." But that wasn't enough. In all his experience he had never heard of Indian trouble that the white man had not started. In this instance the Adjutant General of the Territory felt that the Gutache Mesa killings by Victorio needed a thorough investigation; and under the guise of deputy sheriff, Sack was here to do just that. But she had asked a question.

"I'm a man who looks both ways, miss."

"Clear as mud. But I shouldn't have asked." She eyed him curiously and said, "Back to the robber. You could have taken out after him yesterday afternoon."

"Yes, I could have," Sack said slowly. "Somethin' queer about him, though. First off, I ain't heard of no Sacaton Kid. Next thing, he didn't act like a robber. Took too many chances. Yep, somethin' odd about him. In fact——"

Bonnie waited for a moment. "Go on," she said.

"I was about to say I was hopin' he'd trade my way. But it ain't practical thinkin'."

Bonnie drew in her lower lip and eyed him narrowly before saying: "I know what you mean. Sounds crazy, but I was saying to myself: suppose he does return the money tonight?"

As Sack studied her, his mind sharpened with the possibility that the idea might not be so crazy after all. Then reason told him again that the mind of a hard-headed realist could not harbor such absurd and wishful thinking.

2

SOUTH OF GUTACHE MESA

A MIDMORNING HAZE hung over the mountains and valley when Bonnie saw the town of Bacon in the distance. A mesa cut off the view, though Cactus was driving his six-horse hitch at good speed. The town would next appear between two knolls, and from there the top of the A-T ranch house was visible.

The town lay on the east side of the San Francisco River, Bonnie's house on the other side a quarter-mile northwest in a clump of cottonwoods and sycamores. She could see the crossing now as well as the road leading up to the mining town of Queeny in the canyon, about two miles northeast of Bacon. There were eleven saloons in the tent-and-log town of Queeny with no officer of the law to maintain order. There her father's big mine, the Queeny, dominated the scene. Luke Mason managed it. And right through the mountain lay the Big Beulah Mine belonging to her father's rival, Dan Turrentine.

She glanced back to the settlement of Bacon, its five stores, three saloons, livery barn, and scattered small houses. Near the Frontier Saloon was the stage stop. There her father, and Luke, perhaps, would be waiting to meet her.

Cactus cracked the whip and the yellow wheel jerked forward. The coach was rolling off the incline and clattering toward the saloon before Cactus yelled and braked down hard. The stage stopped abruptly, pitching Bonnie forward. Sack caught her.

She saw Luke through the cloud of dust. He stood near his new buggy, a distant look on his face, a long cheroot in his mouth. His small mustache was right becoming, she admitted again. In fact, Luke had more than a passable face. But something was missing. She could not readily put a finger on it. Then she realized that the Navajo called Indian Joe, almost as constant to Luke as his shadow, was not with him.

The first word she heard spoken upon alighting was, "Posse." Before Luke reached her, she was listening to a man telling another how the Sacaton Kid fanned a six-gun. She scoffed; to hear them talk the robber had shot it out with a dozen men.

Luke took her arm, smiled down at her, saying: "Glad you're home, Bonnie. With stage robbers on the loose and Victorio prizing up hell, it isn't safe for a woman to travel."

"Here I am, safe and sound," she said. "The robber wasn't at all discourteous."

"That's good. But did you hear about the massacre of the two prospectors on Gutache Mesa?"

"Yes," Bonnie replied soberly. "Too bad. Just after they had made a big strike up on Pueblo Creek—so I heard down at the stop."

Luke laughed. "Strike? Burns and Chalmers never hit it big. Just a few nuggets, that's all."

"Depend on you and father to smell out gold," she teased. "But where is father?"

"In the Frontier Saloon. He's talking up a posse. Want to wait for him or ride on to the ranch?"

"I don't know," she said, looking about her. "I wanted to introduce you to the new deputy sheriff, Luke. He's not much to look at, though he seems to have a lot of real horse sense."

"Joe Sack," Luke said. "I met him in Socorro. Remember it was I who went up there for a deputy, Bonnie."

She looked at him, surprised and pleased. "Seems you picked a good man, Luke."

"That's for him to prove to me. But about waiting here, if you don't mind let's go on to the ranch. I've got something on my mind that has to do with you and me."

She knew what he meant, though she said nothing as he

helped her into the buggy. Nor did he broach the subject until the shallow river was behind them. There was nothing boyish or bashful about his approach; he placed the idea before her in a cool businesslike manner that did nothing to stir up any emotion in her: due to growing Indian trouble and the threat of war hanging over the land, he wanted to get married right away.

"What's all that got to do with it?" she asked pointedly.

"Everything. I'll be hard put to keep the mine open for one thing. You know trouble has a way of interfering with the things you want."

"Why, Luke, I believe that's as fine a business proposition as I've ever listened to."

He eyed her sharply for the sarcasm she withheld from her voice and expression. Her glance fell before the scrutiny of his eyes, but not before he saw the mischief at work in her.

"My reasons have nothing to do with my sentiments, Bonnie. You know that."

"I've got your word for it," she said, in matter-of-fact manner.

"Listen, Bonnie. I've missed you a lot, enough to know I want you to marry me without undue delay. Say Sunday week."

She looked at him critically, suppressing a desire to ask if he could spare the time for his wedding. The urge was strong to tell him how nicely Lieutenant Dana danced. Then she was seeing her father's trusted manager and choice of a son-in-law. Dana and the Sacaton Kid held their distance in her mind now that she was home and in Luke's company once more. But there was a good deal missing, things she had not noticed before her trip south. Luke didn't challenge her emotions. For all of his good manners and brilliance and polish, he had not been one tenth as attentive to her in all his courtship as the robber had been with his eyes in the few minutes allotted him.

"I'll think about it," she said.

Luke reined up and the buggy rolled to a stop. His hands drew Bonnie to him. Turning his best face upon her, complimenting her with longing glances, he said: "Think about it now. It means a lot to me, Bonnie."

"Sunday week? No, Luke. I need more time."

A little later the buggy stopped in her own front yard. She was thinking it odd that, though she had returned with three men in mind, only Luke was eligible. Perhaps she was actually closer to marriage with Luke than ever before.

Luke was opening the door for her when she saw her father

and a group of A-T riders approaching. Sack was with them. She waited, thinking it was a weak-looking posse. After her father held her at arm's length and told her how much he had missed her, she remarked on the size of his posse.

McQueen grinned. He was a large genial man in his late forties with sharp blue eyes and graying hair. He looked the part of the big businessman of the Valley since he of the few who had made fortunes here dressed the part. Coat, vest, and string tie were as essential to his dress as boots were to a cowboy. He was saying:

"Joe Sack can handle this thing, Bonnie. He's of the opinion we won't catch the bandit. Better to wait and let him show, which he'll do sooner or later."

Bonnie looked steadily at Sack. Smiling accusingly, she said: "So we're all crazy. Is that it, Mr. Sack?"

"It's a hunch, Miss Bonnie," Sack said defensively. "He may and may not visit these parts. But if he does, we'll spread out to catch him."

"And if he were to return the payroll sack, wouldn't he be square with us?"

Her father chuckled deep. "If the robber is that kind of a fool he ought to hang high."

Bonnie looked fram Sack to her father. "You're both wrong. If the Sacaton Kid shows up, there shouldn't be a man out to stop him from turning honest. And about a hanging—I won't listen to it."

She walked into the house.

McQueen's heavy brows lifted. He tied his horse and said to Mason, "Seem's we got a problem."

"And it ain't Injun trouble," Sack laughed. "Which reminds me of the Gutache Mesa murders. Victorio, I reckon."

"Obviously," Mason replied. "Five years on a reservation, five arrows in a man. It adds up."

"Yeah," Sack said. "I didn't know about that. But it adds up, all right."

McQueen said, "That's not the problem, Luke."

Mason nodded and lit a cigar. As quiet as he was amiable, he seldom gave advice unless it was solicited; and then he hedged about with soft-spoken replies that might vindicate his judgment if he happened to be wrong. After seven years with McQueen, he remained as well respected as upon his arrival. Reserve and patience had made him rich and admired, though he remained unsatisfied in himself, a man with a prodigious ambition at work inside him.

Sack said: "Miss Bonnie may be right about not gettin' in

the Kid's way if he wants to go straight. But I'd be a damn poor deputy not to try and get him."

"Bonnie's high-spirited," McQueen said. "But I don't like to hear her talk in favor of an outlaw."

Mason's eyes narrowed for an instant as he felt a twinge of jealousy and uneasiness. Bonnie had shown an odd streak of independence on the way to the house. She might be putting another man alongside him. A part of him boiled, another part of him laughed it off. He felt secure.

McQueen said, "What would you do, Luke?"

"Don't know." He forced McQueen to place the question again before saying with becoming wisdom, "I might try it both ways, A. T."

"Both ways? What do you mean?"

"You know I'm not good at this sort of thing. Women baffle me. So I humor them. I'd go at it in a way to suit Mr. Sack and Bonnie. Let the outlaw through, if you think he's coming. I don't, and I'll lay odds that he won't. But in case he does, let him come on. Then you've got him trapped. Mr. Sack and a dozen cowboys can ring him in."

This made sense to Sack. He said: "Bein' a deputy I can't gamble on my better judgment, which says he won't come. I've got to think he might do it. And at the same time I've got to give him a chance to hand over the sack if he does come—like Miss Bonnie says. So I like your idea, Luke."

McQueen said: "I've found Luke's judgment pretty reliable. In fact," he added, with a chuckle, "I didn't know I was going to own a mine until Luke told me the Queeny Lode was my property if I wanted it."

Sack looked up, a hand pawing at his mustache. "That's the bonanza a fellow named West discovered, ain't it?"

"The same," Luke replied lazily. "Though there's no record of West's claim on file. When he was found with an arrow in his back, I staked it for A. T. He had the operating capital. I didn't."

"Luke just put up the mining brains in the partnership," McQueen laughed. "But you seem to know a lot about this country, Sack. Ever been here before?"

"Nope. Just poked through the records at the courthouse and asked a lot of questions here'n there." He looked at Mason and said: "But about this outlaw. Seems you hit on the right idea in this matter. Much obliged."

Luke Mason pretended surprise at having solved the problem. He said, with the air of a man under jest by smarter men, "You two had that figured out ahead of me, and you know it."

He took the few steps to his buggy and said: "I'm due back at the mine. Turrentine is within eighty feet of our side of the hill and he's angling in on the Blind Monk Canyon side."

McQueen knit his brows and rubbed his chin. "This Turrentine business—if trouble is smokin' up there, I'd better talk to Big Dan. Maybe we can settle this thing."

"Not yet, A. T. He's on his claim now. But if he crosses his line by so much as one inch, we'll tie him up in court."

Luke climbed into the buggy and, seeing McQueen's look of satisfaction, glanced at Sack.

"Don't hang the outlaw before you catch him, Mr. Sack."

Sack nodded and watched Mason drive off. He was wondering how it happened to be Luke who traveled all the way to Socorro for a deputy; and just what made Luke Mason tick, actually.

And Mason was driving toward Queeny and Beulah Orbon who operated the Green Palace Hotel, asking just what kind of deputy sheriff Sack would turn out to be. A man he could dominate, or the stubborn kind?

He shrugged it off and called up an image of Beulah's dark eyes and soft red lips. She was more interesting in that he knew her intimately and yet really knew nothing at all of what was within her. A tall long-limbed woman of fine figure and poise, she was the item of contention between him and Dan Turrentine, who had named his mine Big Beulah after her. Big Dan could operate in the open in his pursuit of her. On account of Bonnie, Luke couldn't. Which failed to shake Luke's confidence. Nothing affected that quality in Luke Mason. Beulah knew this. In a way it kept her jumping, even as it did Bonnie.

But Turrentine was in the way. Often of late Mason had dropped casual remarks about the saloons, and to McQueen that hinted of trouble, far off and growing, trouble caused by a hill between Queeny Canyon and the Blind Monk. If and when it came, over Beulah, it would be about something else. And it was coming, though it wouldn't reach any court.

Near the mouth of the canyon, a lone Apache crossed the road not a dozen yards ahead. As peaceful as you please, Luke was thinking. He stopped the horse and gazed thoughtfully after the savage. Then he caught himself about to speak to his Navajo. He laughed. Indian Joe was several miles south on a little errand.

18

3

THE RIDER OF THE NIGHT

DARKNESS HAD SETTLED over the Valley when A-T riders caught and held Bonnie's attention. They moved in muffled trot in every direction.

She stood on the porch, in the same place where her father and Sack came upon her at about ten minutes of nine. Having listened to Luke's compromise plan, as related by her parent, and finding it practical enough to silence her, she had watched them enter the bunkhouse without any protest. Sack had a job to do, she admitted resentfully. But her silence was no indication of how she felt about it. In the dark the tight lines of her face didn't show.

First, Luke had struck off for Queeny instead of standing by her while she disposed of an odd situation—if the robber came—in her own way. By scoffing at an impossibility, she thought he was ignoring her. Next, she was left alone with a growing fear that should the Kid materialize, the urge of a dozen men to shoot would find outlet in at least one of them.

Silence was by now a negative, light thing. Then it seemed packed with urgency, seemed to call upon her to do something, to accept what might come with total indifference. She thought of the robber and smiled. He would not come here. He had no reason to risk it, had every reason not to.

She had turned to go inside the house when a rider entered the yard.

"Who is it?" she said.

"Southworth, Percy Southworth. Quite new at the A-T Station, y'know, Miss Bonnie."

"Station?" she asked as the cowboy rode up. Then she knew. He was the English cowboy just in from Australia. "You gave me a start," she said. "But why aren't you with the others?"

"We spread out, y'know. Well, a stranger just rode past me toward the horse paddock. When I said, 'I say, who goes there?' the chap introduces himself with a pistol and remarks in quite contained voice, as though he were inviting me to sit and boil a billy of tea, 'Tell Bonnie McQueen to call the riders in. I'm coming to the house.'"

"Then—it's the Sacaton Kid!"

19

"Quite accurate, Miss Bonnie. That's what he said. I was put in a ludicrous state of fluster when I heard his name, I assure you. Shall I call in the others?"

"Go to Mr. Sack. Tell him I said to warn the men against any shooting. And I mean it!"

As the cowboy galloped off into the night, Bonnie stood still and tense. So he had come. She couldn't understand it. And he had asked for the riders, all bandit chasers now, to return. It simply failed to make sense. Shaking it off with a toss of her head, she went inside and returned with a lantern. She had no sooner placed it on the porch hook than a voice out of the night caused her to whirl.

"Hello, Bonnie."

He was walking into the yellow lantern light with the pay-roll sack. Placing it on the porch, he looked up at her, examining her as though he liked all he saw.

An uncalled-for silence gripped her. Words wouldn't come, and she just stood there unable to believe he had come here. All the while she was seeing his face for the first time. The eyes she had seen, but not the long muscular mouth, now set in a humorous line, or the strong chin and jaws and straight nose. He was the color of bronze and well dressed. She sensed a clean strong pride in him. Maybe he wasn't the robber. The sandy hair and the pair of eyes said he was.

She found her voice. "You're a fool to come here," she said. "I had no idea you'd do it."

"What about that trap you set, Bonnie?"

Aware that no explanation would sound convincing, she said, "Why did you do it?"

"Because that was part of my plan before I robbed the stage."

She stared incredulously and sized him up again. This time for a fool. But the memory of his calm of yesterday was poignantly fresh. He was a copy of it now. His chill eyes showed no sign of disturbance. He might be a poke on a chuck line or a notorious gambler, though she could not deny that the open West had stamped him with its brand of self-reliance and vigilance. He was baffling.

"Perhaps you don't know what happens to stage robbers around here," she said. "They hang. Why don't you leave while you can?"

"Thanks. But that isn't a part of my plan." His intent look held. He was taken by her large eyes, the directness and challenge and fear for his safety in them. The timbre of her voice, rich and low, attracted and excited him now as much as it had in memory. He was thinking these things and his look told her as much.

Her glance slid away, out into the night where running horses came on at full gallop.

"Very well," she said. "It's your funeral."

He put his back to her and hung his thumbs in belt as the tattoo of hoofs drew closer. She was looking from the A-T riders getting off their horses in the yard back to him with a growing uneasiness. Her father and Sack dismounted and walked toward the porch wary and poised. An electric air hung over the scene, a split second away from either peace or powder smoke. Nothing happened and McQueen and Sack, backed by the riders, stood a few yards away.

Still Young appeared as calm as a guest for dinner. Bonnie followed the direction of his steady gaze, upon her father, who studied the robber intently. She looked from one to the other as their glance held strong and unsettling, each digging deep into the other's eyes.

Sack was saying: "Well, Kid, I've seen all kinds of men, but you take the cake. Didn't think you'd do it, much less hang around for a reception committee."

Young made no reply.

McQueen said, "So this is the Sacaton Kid." It was neither a question nor a statement, but an expression of his regard for outlaws in general. "All right, Sack. It's up to you now."

Bonnie said: "You're wrong, father. He returned the payroll money, so we're all square."

"It's not that easy, Bonnie. He broke the law, robbed, and shot. Just because he turned yellow and sneaked back here with it don't mean he won't try it again. A robber is a thief, same as a polecat is a skunk."

The A-T foreman chuckled out loud. At his signal the punchers laughed.

Young broke the dead expression of his face and said, "That's about what I expected of you, McQueen."

His voice was conversationally low and controlled and his eyes were steady, too steady and icy, thought Sack, who took a step between the pair only to face Young's gun as it came up with incredible speed.

"Don't interfere now, Mr. Sack, "Young said, adding, "If you please. Nor any of the rest of you out there."

Seconds later, he replaced his pistol and said: "You don't know who I am, McQueen. It goes back a few years. That's why I robbed you of your payroll and rode here to return it."

McQueen was naturally puzzled. He could not guess at the robber's identity.

"My name is Young West."

"I never heard of you," McQueen said.

"But you have heard of John Hammond West, haven't you? He discovered the claim you've been working for several years. He was my father, McQueen."

Surprise was written across McQueen's face.

"So that's it," he said. "Well, young fellow, everybody around here knows what happened to West. Victorio's Apaches got him."

"Victorio and his Apaches were on San Carlos Reservation at the time," Young said. "To further prove they didn't get him, he wasn't mutilated. And they didn't take his rifle or horse."

"What's that got to do with me?"

"Maybe you can explain it," Young said.

McQueen stiffened. "Why should I explain anything to you?"

"You got rich off my father's discovery. Now suppose you prove you got it fair and square."

"Young man," came the controlled reply, "why don't you try and prove I didn't?"

"I am," Young said.

McQueen was angry. "You've got a gall," he said, "coming to my place with that kind of talk. All I've got to do is lift a finger to turn my men loose on a stage robber."

"I'm taking that chance," came the quiet reply.

Sack stepped between them, saying: "Tighten rein, boys, and step off the powder keg. You're both right and both wrong."

Sack's intervention did nothing to thin the air. Bonnie felt helpless under the weight of fresh discovery that the Kid who was Young West was almost accusing her father of murder and theft. But Sack was talking:

"West, your old man prospected from the Organs to the High Sierras. He came out here, struck it rich. They found him dead, face down in the creek with an arrow in his back. If he had filed a claim, McQueen couldn't legally work the Queeny diggin's."

"The first thing he would have done is file a claim, Mr. Sack. But there's no record of it. However, we know that records have been tampered with before."

"You're talkin' mighty strong, Kid," Sack warned.

"That's what I came here for," Young said. "I'm looking for the murderer, and I'm giving McQueen a chance to help me find him if he's innocent."

Sack said: "And under threat. Sure. You're born for ven-

22

geance. Alive today, dead tomorrow. That frame of mind won't take you far, Kid. But let me get this straight—is that the reason you took McQueen's payroll?"

"That's right."

"Why did you go at it that way, Kid?"

"To let him know I mean business."

"Well, you took the wrong way," Sack said. "And I ought to jail you for robbery, just to save you from your own blasted hot head. If I don't, the folks around here may string up a robber."

He looked at McQueen. "A. T., the Kid has proved beyond a shadow of a doubt that the motive weren't robbery. He brought in the payroll, so I'm advisin' that, since no jury would convict him of robbery, you'd be smart not to press charges."

"He's square with us," Bonnie said firmly.

"All right," McQueen said. "But he'd better not cross my path again.

Charlie Wyatt spoke up. "Maybe he'd better put some distance between him and these parts."

"I'm staying around until I find out who got my father," Young said.

"Which ain't smart," Sack advised.

Young moved toward his horse. In the saddle, he looked at Bonnie. Her fixed gaze was upon him, strong with curiosity and bewilderment, and more. Somewhere in her face or behind it he saw and felt interest and challenge at work. He lingered a moment, just to return whatever it was she gave, then sent his horse toward the river at a slow trot.

Bonnie's gaze followed Young until the night closed him off. When she looked for her father, he was nowhere about. Only Sack stood there, his face alerted as he watched Wyatt, who was talking in low tones among his men. Soon the riders walked their horses toward the corral and she walked up to Sack with extended hand.

"You handled it nicely," she said. "I was looking for all sorts of trouble. Let's hope there won't be any."

He took her hand and said nothing. He blew out his cheeks, which was his way of restraining a bellowing voice and advice he wanted to cram into her head: "Hell, girl, that's foolish hopin'! It's like the 'Pache trouble, just begun!"

Then he turned toward the house.

Alone, Bonnie looked toward the river. She was soon in the saddle riding down the road to Bacon. Ahead, a lone horseman drew up and listened. She rode on.

Young put his gun away when he recognized her. She drew

up alongside him where they waited out a tense silence. She broke it, saying:

"I've been thinking about your reason for coming here. It might be better if you were a stage robber."

He said nothing.

"I followed you because I don't want any more trouble," she said. "You and father got off to a bad start. I'm sure he'll help you find the guilty person when he cools off. And you weren't exactly friendly, coming here as you did."

"I wanted your father to know I was dead serious. I still am. And if he can't see it my way, next time I'll——"

"There won't be a next time, Young West."

Taken unexpectedly, he stared at her. Then he was measuring the recklessness and command in her firm reply. With her so near, he saw these things and courage too behind her composed expression; even in the dim light of night he saw them rise up with speculation and judgment and eagerness in her; as though she felt duty bound to fashion the fabric of his destiny. He didn't like the idea of a McQueen's interference, though he did like her directness. He could not help that.

"Just what are you going to do?" she said.

"Haven't had time to think about it."

"Take time," she demanded.

Something about her went through him like a drink of strong wine. He fought the clamor of his pulses and clung fast to the things he could think of clearly.

"I'm going to find out who shot my father."

"You should have done that first. Now just what else are you going at backwards?"

"Suppose your father had a hand in it?"

"You're mighty sure of that," she said.

"What would you think if you were in my place, Bonnie?"

She looked up at the summer stars as if they had overtaken her, trapped her into a state of incertitude. Her voice was less calm when she said, "I'm sure father had no part in it." When she spoke next there was a sharp edge to her low voice. "And I'll fight against you. Young West, as hard as I've fought for you, if you want it that way—until you prove he did."

"Then we'll leave it that way," he said, nudging his horse forward.

A burning anger flowed in him, made worse by the knowledge that it wasn't entirely justified. But she wasn't at all wise in thinking she could dominate him on the strength of her desire for peace.

They rode on to the edge of the river and let the horses drink. This was the parting place. She knew it and he knew

24

it, and she realized that the ruse was thin when she said her saddle was loose. But she was thinking that he must cool off and look at trouble as something to avoid. What she felt was different, a personal indignation of neglect and a tremble of hurt, then a rush of anger to her brain. Against feuds and the men who refused to meet peace halfway. But these were all mere advance emotions to the one she was trying to suppress.

He was standing by her saddle with a hand on the horn. A vast sense of weakness in her was followed by a warm surge of blood that beat life into her pulses. She was drawn to him, fighting back, trying her utmost to restrain the hand that was falling to his.

She managed to draw her hand away, though he was not of the same mind. The touch of her fingers went through him like fire, and he grasped her hand, looked up into her face, searching for all that it gave and all that it withheld. He saw a pair of eyes gazing into his, unguardedly. Excitement stirred in them, vaguely in the pale mask of evening, but enough for expression. She was talking to him without spoiling what she said with inadequate words, telling him how she felt, asking if he could feel it as well.

He could not remember afterward how he drew her out of the saddle, whether she came or whether he lifted her bodily to the earth. But she was standing before him and his arms were drawing her closer to him. Her head went back and she stared into his face with trust and entreaty in her shining glance.

Her mouth was soft when he touched it. Warm and alive and like the hot winds that formed and whirled about him and through him, possessing him completely. And she returned all that he gave with clinging eagerness and little contented sighs. With the break, he seemed to know, as she did, that they were fused into one spiritual being. No matter what might follow this night, trouble or pain or broken ties, or open enmity between them, what had been done could never be undone.

She stepped back from him. He stood stock still looking at her, wondering what she had done to him, if he would ever again be the same. Everything seemed swept aside, as in a desert flood in which arroyos run rampant with water for a few hours today and look up dusty at the sun tomorrow. Then he was saying things he had no intention of saying:

"So you'd fight against me, Bonnie. I could take that payroll sack and hole up in some canyon and tell you where. You'd do nothing against me. Not you, Bonnie McQueen."

The next thing he knew he was standing with thumbs in

25

belt, frowning as though suddenly awake and aware of what he had said.

He got into the saddle and sat there for a few seconds. Then he said, "So long, Bonnie."

She watched him go, heard the splashing in the shallows until it suddenly ceased. A muted shuffle of hoofs, a casual gait, and all sound died. He was gone. Still she stood there, motionless, knowing that nothing must happen to him.

4

EXIT THE SACATON KID

YOUNG RODE STRAIGHT for the lights of Bacon. Bonnie was too much in his mind for any clear thinking, and he rode on beyond the town for a time, feeling in fresh memory her clinging hands at his neck and the sweet pressure of her lips. But she was deeper than touch, and he was looking into her mind, at purpose which matched his in strength, and the firm decision in her that spoke in threat and entreaty in a bid for peace. And he knew her to be right. Like Sack, the things she said were for his own good. Trouble was easy to find.

He felt the presence of it as he tied his horse before the Frontier Saloon; a number of A-T horses were there ahead of him.

He entered the saloon and looked it over. The bar ran down the right wall. Behind it a big mirror framed in gingerbread work was flanked by shelves and open stained-glass doors, and topped with pictures, the largest of which was an artist's conception of the Battle of Gettysburg. Young took these things in at a glance, as he did the fat barman with a black club beard, the tables about which men played poker and talked and drank.

Suddenly he realized that all eyes had turned on him.

Only one face was familiar. It was big-boned and full with stretched thin lips under a sweat-circled range hat. Young felt a sense of sharp warning as he met Charlie Wyatt's glance, seeing in it a shrewd and ominous perversity at work. The A-T foreman had already warned him to "put some distance between him and these parts."

Young moved carelessly to the bar through hanging layers of smoke. The black eyes of the barman dug into his as he ordered a drink, and continued to gaze at him for a second or two. Then the barman broke the quiet with a question:

"What about it, Charlie?"

"The man asked for a drink, Jase," Wyatt said, in a slow pleasant drawl.

Jason Muench placed a bottle and a small glass on the bar. Young poured slowly, lifted the glass, with his left hand, turned about and said, "Thanks, Charlie."

Wyatt said nothing, though the humoring smile left his face. He sat still, his bull chest lifting and falling. His men caught on, and Young saw them move slowly away from the bar until he was the only man between the crowd and the mirror. A little man moved to the yellow-white piano in a corner, looked at the keys, raised his hands, then apparently thought better of it, until Charlie Wyatt said:

"Go ahead and play, Big Man. Something sad like."

An old bearded man jumped up and asked for a song. A laugh followed, and soon a man said: "Sure, Big Man. Loco Tom will give you a piece of solid silver rock from his secret vein."

Then Charlie Wyatt told them to leave Loco Tom alone. Big Man hit a chord and found his way. Young downed his drink in a gulp, paid for it, surveying the crowd through the mirror. Then he turned around.

"Ask him who he is, Jase," Wyatt said.

"Who are you?" the barman asked.

"Young West."

"Ask him if he ain't the Sacaton Kid, Jase."

Young propped elbows on the bar lip and said: "Tell him I was, Jase. But not any more."

"Tell him, Jase, what happens to stage robbers out here."

"They hang."

Young smiled. "It's a small world. They hang where I come from, too."

Wyatt said: "Jase, tell him we don't want no trouble, that we got a rope handy and anxious, that he has a ten-minute start. As of right now."

Young was quick to reply. "Jase, tell him I don't scare easily. I came out here to find out who got my old man and I'm not leaving until I settle the score."

Wyatt glanced lazily from him to the watch he held. A minute ticked by, then another, each of which was marked by Wyatt's warning.

"Tell him he's got nine minutes left, Jase. Tell him he's got eight minutes, Jase."

Seven minutes had slipped away when the man next to

27

Wyatt got up and walked outside. He returned shortly with a lariat rope.

"Throw it over the rafter, Bugs," Wyatt ordered. "Jase, tell him he's got one minute left."

"Hell, not in here! Hell, no!" Jase protested.

"In here, Jase, where we can all see it," Wyatt said, in humoring but firm tones.

The rope swung over the center beam and the tall poke called Bugs tested it with his weight.

"Now, Jase, tell him his time's up."

"The hell! Tell him yourself, Charlie."

Young's expression had not changed. With a calm that seemed too controlled, a little disconcerting to the crowd and to Charlie Wyatt's men in particular, he faced them as if he were a mere spectator at their proposed hanging. Then he glanced lazily at the rafter. What happened next was a little too fast for the eye.

His gun came up. A shot sounded and the rope fell in two pieces.

Jase Muench's bellowing voice had a placating ring in it as he said: "Drinks on the house, boys! Line up! Hit the keys, Big Man!"

Charlie Wyatt annulled the invitation. He said nothing, all he did then was stand up with feet pushed apart and thumbs in his belt. It was enough. His eyes were thin and fixed on Young; they flashed and a cold light played in them, a lusting challenge that seemed to demand a shedding of blood. Slowly his elbows bent upward until his arms were straight out from the massive shoulders and his hands were hovering a foot out from his two guns. He was hunching over, mouth slack, eyes boring, when Young, still calm, elbows on the bar lip, said easily:

"Tell him he's making a mistake, Jase."

"Hell, yes, you are, Charlie! I can tell! The Kid's too calm!"

Young was anything but calm inside, though excitement in him sprang from effect instead of cause: he was weighing the value of victory over McQueen's foreman and finding it wholly unedifying. To shoot Charlie Wyatt would brand him forever the Sacaton Kid. The town wouldn't have it otherwise. His mind was made up.

He said: "I reckon he wins, Jase. Take my guns."

An oath of surprise, scorn, and unslaked desire fell from Wyatt's lips.

"Damn yellow!" he said. "All yellow! Gut deep yellow.

28

Calm, you say, Jase? Just scared. So we'll get on with it. Knot the rope, Jones, and hit the rafter. On the first try."

From the back of the room a commanding voice was heard: "Just a minute, Wyatt."

Young had not seen Sack move through the batwing door. But there he stood rubbing his red mustache, arresting all movement in the saloon.

"The new deputy," Bugs laughed before throwing the rope over the rafter.

Sack walked slowly up to the bar. He looked at Young, then Wyatt, and said slowly, convincingly: "Charlie, a man has a right to think what he wants to about a man who won't draw with him. And about a stagecoach robber. Your opinion is good as mine. But I'm sayin' this. The Kid here would of dusted you on both sides, expert and proper, before you touched guns. And why he didn't weren't yellow. It was good judgment."

Wyatt laughed. "Yeah. Damn good judgment. But yellow all the same. First he robs the stage, then scares and returns the money. Then he bluffs it up before A. T. with a lot of threats. He was hidin' behind Miss Bonnie. But she ain't here, so he ups and quits when I call his bluff. And he ain't yellow, you say?"

"That's what I say, Charlie," Sack replied, in a voice that wiped the grins off faces in the crowd. "What's more, I guarantee it."

"That ought to be enough," Wyatt said, pushing his hat back on his head. "Seein' as how it comes from the man Luke Mason picked for deputy sheriff."

As the crowd responded to this surprise with rising conversation, Wyatt said in loud edged voice: "But it don't. Not quite, it don't. 'Cause it just don't make sense."

"All right," Sack said. "Granted it don't make good sense, that's what it is. You heard the Kid say he was John Hammond West's boy. We all know West was arrowed just after he struck pay dirt up at Queeny. The Kid wants to know who done it, same as you or me would."

"Hell, Victorio done it!" Wyatt argued hotly.

"Charlie, you heard the Kid say Victorio's tribes was on reservation at the time. I'm sayin' it's the truth. Look it up yourself."

Sack went on: "So, you see, he can't do much lookin' around if he's outlawed. And if he put a slug twixt your eyes, Charlie, the folks around here would of outlawed him quicker'n you could bulldog a three-legged maverick in a Texas blue norther."

Pausing, he added: "So it took guts to make like he was yellow, Charlie."

Wyatt nodded, and shook his head, perplexed. Shrugging his big shoulders, he said: "Well, even if I ain't satisfied about the guts of a stage robber, the drinks are on me. Line up, every last damn man of you—even the stage robber."

So saying, he dropped a hand fast. In the split second his gun roared. The rope Bugs had thrown over the rafter for the second time was cut in half once more.

He looked at Young, and there was nothing friendly in his glance; just challenge deep and undisguised.

Later that night, Young drew Sack aside and said: "Seems I owe a lot to you, Mr. Sack. First you let the stage bandit go free. Now you've stopped me from hanging by a rope or running for it. Why did you do it?"

"I like the way you fan a gun and the way you used your head with Wyatt, Kid. A man who can do them two things might come in handy when the time comes."

Young said nothing and Sack looked intently at him for some time before saying: "I hadn't been in this town five minutes when I learned something new about that Gutache Mesa massacre. I can't talk about it yet, no matter how it stinks."

Young looked puzzled. "If I can ever repay you, call——"

Sack interrupted: "Kid, if what I think is true, I will call on you. But I'm warnin' you it will be a helluva lot bigger hunt than the one you're on now."

5

THE MARK OF VICTORIO

AT ABOUT THE TIME Sack was telling Young this, a courier from Fort Bayard got off his horse at a small outpost southeast of Gila Crossing and asked for Lieutenant Dana.

"In the castle there," came the reply.

The courier looked wise. The long adobe huts surrounded by a hip-high wall of rocks made up Fort Mangus. He knew the joke at Bayard: if an officer offended the high brass they sent him to Fort Mangus. He knew also that First Lieutenant Goodell Dana had done just that.

Lieutenant Dana met the courier with a semblance of hope

30

in his tight face. The officers' ball at Bayard tomorrow evening was uppermost in his mind as he broke the seal on the dispatch. Then he was reading the order from General Bent, jaws working into crawling ridges and hard flashes shooting about in his eyes. He was still the high cockalorum of Mangus, for the order said:

> Proceed to Lieutenant Botts's camp on Gutache
> Mesa with haste.

There was more: the General hoped to avoid mounting a full campaign; the Lieutenant should contact a Mr. Joe Sack, who was secretly investigating the Gutache Mesa affair for the Adjutant General of the Territory; the Lieutenant should hold his troop intact on the march, work amiably with Lieutenant Botts until Captain Corday arrived to assume command.

So it was to be Captain Corday again. Such luck shouldn't happen to an officer.

Alone, he glanced at the dispatch again, kicked a chair, and called in a loud voice for Sergeant Reeder, who entered almost at once.

"As you were, Reeder," he snapped.

The Sergeant was big and gaunt, but sullen in Dana's presence; had been since the Mescalero campaign. But so had others from corporals up to the Colonel, even the General.

"Troop A is moving up above the town of Bacon. Tonight." He gave detailed orders about the token force to be left behind and other things, then said, "That's all, Reeder."

But that wasn't all; his mind was ticking over slowly with reports out of Bacon and Queeny. Conditions were none too good up there. What with the lawlessness and flowing whisky, it was small wonder that more Indians didn't hit the warpath. Horses were being stolen and cabins burned. The military overlooked these small things.

And now two prospectors had died with burning arrows in them. Five in each. Somehow, Dana felt it, the Army was in for more than it realized.

A little later, Troop A hit the saddle, jogged out, pushed stolidly north toward the Gila River through the sheen of night, carbines laxed, yellow neckerchiefs dim in the starlight. A glum outfit that looked ahead to saddle sores and the eternal chase of an enemy who wasn't there. This was the Mangus troop. The General was a benevolent man.

The General knew the Army, but not the Apache. From Colorado, he was tame-minded, Ute and Arapahoe influenced.

Dana rode at the head of the column, looking straight

31

ahead, thinking of the past, never forgetting that he was in a rut, long steps from promotion. He had won disfavor in the Mescalero campaign a few months back because he led his men into a trap, lost a dozen, and, most of all, because he had been right in the strategy that finally saved Troop C and the battle. But he had been dressed down because he failed to run when Captain Corday's trumpeter bounced retreat off the crags. That was the Army. Better to be wrong and obedient than win a victory against orders.

Though he wasn't the kind to smart under yesterday's discipline, blame for a scout's error went against the grain. Young West, the scout, was on the peak late one afternoon looking at White Moon's war party, at Corday's and Dana's. He was there heliographing Corday, telling him of the line of march of White Moon and Dana. But Corday marched on away from the trap he, Dana, had planned. Toward dawn, West rode up and said the attack would come from the south. It didn't. And when Corday's trumpet blew retreat there was no place to go.

He wouldn't forget this Young West.

That campaign was the close past. This one, if it could be called that, lay ahead, up and over weary miles of cactus, yucca, and parched land, up in the manzanita perhaps; all because two prospectors tempted Victorio's braves and died with five arrows in each of them.

Prospecting, the intelligence said. But was it something else? Somebody was cunning and sharp up at Queeny or Bacon. Was it guns and liquor? It stank even as it smelled Apache and a man held his nose and he didn't; he got used to it, like he did dust. But where white men gathered there was Indian trouble. They lied and cheated and nobody's word was good.

The hell with it, he shot back into the empty night.

The officers' ball was tomorrow night and the pretty McQueen girl would be there. Bonnie had smiled at hero Corday. And tomorrow night while Corday danced with her, he would be lying flat of his back gazing up at empty stars with smells of sweat and leather in the air instead of Bonnie's perfume.

But that was a hot-head's fate. A lieutenant until they broke you for more hot-headedness. Ten years of it, he, Senator Tom Dana's boy from Virginia, kicked out of school early for the sweet little temper he humored. He should have red hair, though it was brown and wavy. He should own a pair of beady gray eyes, but they were soft and brown. He was fashioned a contradiction.

He fell back to the column. "All right, Sergeant Reeder.

This isn't quite the time to show trail-lousy. The General said, 'with haste.' "

Sergeant Reeder said something, inarticulate though conforming. Dana didn't hear what he said next—"Bastard of a loo-tenant!" He was thinking of Bonnie McQueen again, seeing in memory a woman with life in her fine face and figure. She challenged all men. Only one would win her. And hadn't he as much right to dance with her at Fort Bayard as the other officers? He had, though General Bent thought otherwise.

"Proceed with haste," he scowled into the night. What the General meant, actually was:

> *On to Gila, Mr. Dana, but don't stop there. Go on up where it's dry and hot and desolate. Smell dust and look at beargrass and yucca and rocks as they saw into the flesh and bruise you. Shake out your boots, if you ever take them off, Mr. Dana— if you can—there might be a whip scorpion in one of them. Dry poison, Mr. Dana.*

It was the Army. He hated it, loved it; all one hundred and eighty-five pounds of his five feet and eleven inches was used to it and all that it could hand a man from battle to promotion, to the Sixty-Fourth Article of War.

He rode down the line and prodded his men awake. He cursed and turned his head north again, oblivious to the stars, the slow shuffle of hoofs, or the distant wail of a coyote. A light far ahead appeared on a mountain slope. It went out. Another sprang up. Before morning, Victorio would know how many troopers were on the march up to the 'Frisco Valley. It was uncanny, but it was so.

For a moment he was wondering if the five arrows in each of the prospectors on Gutache Mesa were meant to convey something.

A shiver ran up his spine.

Toward noon next day, Lieutenant Dana rubbed his grim face with a gauntleted hand and halted his troop. A big Queeny freight wagon drawn by six mules ground to a halt. The grizzled old wagoner spat tobacco juice and spoke of the Gutache killings:

"Danged 'Paches didn't touch the corn or sowbelly in the wagon, so says Lieutenant Botts. And the horses wasn't took nor killed. Odd as hell, I says. Ain't the 'Pache way."

He talked on: Botts reported that it looked like the work of one Indian, since only the tracks of one pony could be found. And that pony wore shoes, also uncommon to Apache ponies. And the left front horseshoe was larger than the other three.

Then he slung whip and roared at his mules and creaked on south, leaving Dana lost in thought.

With many lame horses, Troop A moved on at a walk, spur rowels jingling, shuffling up dust. It was dismount and lead, a general halt every hour on through the hot long miles over Cactus Flat. They moved at a snail's pace when the order was, "Proceed with haste."

The Flat seemed long and endless. The wagoner's tale clung leechlike to Dana's brain all that afternoon.

He wiped sweat with his yellow neckerchief and felt the grime cutting into his face like pumice. Sweat-caked and smelly, rather a part of the trailing smell of men and horses, he pulled his tunic out from wet skin and trudged on. He was wishing for rain, a downpour. Which, he snorted in disgust, was like wishing he were on the banks of the Potomac with a whiskey julep in one hand and a lady's delicate fingers in the other. The dream died and he saw smelly greasewood, prickly pear, ground bush, and dry yellow dirt. An antelope halted ahead, curious, and out of range. A vermilion flycatcher flew by. The sun painted the crags of a canyon in deep orange. The sky was still a brass reflector of heat that furred the distant range. Ahead, all ahead, was ambush country.

As the troop marched down off the Flat into the first blind curve of Big Dry road, Dana felt fear down the line of his column. It was downhill all the way in short, stiff-legged steps, carbines ready, in elbow-crook, troop alert. It was a treacherous road, patterned after hairpins and fingernails; it hung against dry walls and flirted with sheer drops down into purpling draws. One more hell of a road.

In sharp contrast, the day was fading away beautifully. An evening daze dominated all distances, broken only by a colorful sky and glints of orange on the Mogollon crags. A vagrant breeze stirred, whisked on above the walls of the road like a song burdened with somber, ageless things a man wanted to hear and then didn't.

Dana scowled. Something told him not to go on. Across the miles of wasteland the maw of Big Dry Canyon glowed in orange like a rhinoceros afire. He felt alone and no amount of glaring back at the damned canyon could lessen his growing presentiment.

He fell back and said to Reeder: "Sergeant, we split here. I'll take a detail of twelve and skirt ahead." Even as he said it, General Bent's crisp, incisive voice rang in his ears: "Hold intact on the march, Lieutenant."

Then he said, sternly impatient: "All right, men—Turner, O'Berry, Booker, Yeager, Hutch, Bartlett, Diaz, Bennett, Chaves, Black, Goldsmith, and Harwood—fall in! No horses, just rifles and sharp eyes. Turner and O'Berry to the ridges. Flank the road ahead, low crouch, and ready!"

Fear of attack was of short duration, he told himself. The Apache didn't strike after dark, in fear of his wandering ghosts. A man could sleep well. But the dawn was early and dangerous. The dusk was late and just as ominous.

O'Berry moved on, swore at the Lieutenant when he thought he was out of earshot. Dana heard and didn't hear; he had been a trooper once. Then O'Berry returned and said there was no Indian sign anywhere; but he smelled water in the Dry.

"Peel your eyes, Turner. Fail to find Indian sign when it's there and your blood will turn to ice water." A man learned that on his first campaign. He didn't have to learn it twice.

The wagon massacre on Gutache Mesa preyed in Dana's mind. The prospectors had hit it rich up on Pueblo Creek, so the old wagoner had said; McQueen had tried to buy them out; and trouble was brewing between McQueen and a mine-owner named Turrentine. Therefore, Dana thought on, if the Apache massacre was as phony as it sounded, a mining feud might be all he was marching to.

Shapes were losing detail in the falling mantle of evening. A deep purple thickened the air. Soon, very soon, night would fall. Then they could march on or throw the spider on the fire and sit out the smell of frying bacon. No need for putting out fires or muting a trumpet.

Then it was dark of a sudden, black dark until their eyes got used to it. Dana called the scouts in and waited out Reeder's approach. Then he ordered the march to continue. Reeder asked how far; he knew this hill; there was a spot around a curve where Major Fremont camped several years ago.

"No water," Dana replied.

Reeder laughed in the dark; his first hint of insolence, Dana thought. "The San Francisco is a long way off, sir."

"And wet," Dana replied, with warning in his voice.

To which the Sergeant wanted to say that the paymaster's ambulance at the rear carried a barrel of water for the horses, that the men could suffer quarter rations because the command hadn't the gumption to replenish on the Gila. But he said nothing of the kind, just worked up precious saliva, defiantly, and spat it with a noisy show of independence.

Dana was wise. He smiled, and thought Reeder a good man

to have along in case of attack. Troop A reached Little Dry Creek and found caked mud, nothing more. The horses sniffed and looked up before lowering their heads again to the craving smell. A fire lit up the night in quick time. The flames painted dusty men, all hungry.

The spider was on the fire, horses were picketed; and a dozen men were assigned to the troop guard and listening posts ordered extended out.

Then it happened. Something unheard of, and Dana didn't believe it, since the Apache of this country had never been known to violate his black-of-night rule of no attack.

But there was Turner—a moment before singing as he squatted before the fire—rising to his feet with a stunned look of horror on his face, staring unbelievingly at an arrow in the middle of his belly. Then he let out a scream that faded out in the anguish of despair, and Dana knew he felt no pain but that complete resignation to the inevitable.

And Dana, who had seen men die before, had no time for compassion. He was churning his brain with position and defense, with the un-Apache paradox even as he leaped for the rifles and shouted commands. But it was schooled experience that issued orders, and not he, for his mind was groping for some key to the Apache mystery and it was directing one ear, tuning it, to the expected yells from out in the night. The other ear awaited the thud of Turner's body as it hit the ground.

Turner slipped to the ground silently, his eyes staring in death. And all was quiet for a moment or two, too quiet. Then suddenly another arrow fell, quivered near the fire. The next came seconds later. Trooper Diaz caught it. The tip stuck out behind his neck, the feather trembling before his very eyes. Diaz fell, clawing at the thing frantically.

Three arrows. Two men gone. Dana fired into the night. The order to charge the unseen enemy was changed to "Scatter!"

A man screamed in the dark, flailed about noisily, and his voice was unnaturally calm as he said, "It's me, Booker. Right in the middle."

Guns barked and bullets whined, spat hard against trees and rocks and died. Then Reeder's crisp voice, rattling off orders expertly from unexcited lips, cried out, "Through my forearm!"

Troop A waited for the big attack, taut, sharp-eyed, staring into the darkness over rifles, Reeder obliquely off the south road, Dana on the north, nobody in the blacked-out camp. Troop A continued to wait. Waited for nothing.

And Lieutenant Dana thinking over and over again: "Five arrows: The mark of Victorio!" Thinking also: "It's not like the Apache. All arrows came from the same direction, from one bow, perhaps. And at night. It isn't the Apache way."

There was little sleep in camp that night. The troop was on the move before dawn, with three dead men in the paymaster's ambulance. On the column plodded, a grim, scared bunch of troopers who were wishing the dawn would not slide up in the morning sky that day. The dawn belonged to the Apache.

Lieutenant Dana felt the onus of command. Every name on the roll and horse book was his responsibility. Three men were dead. That added up. The night attack didn't. But together they were the two and two that made four. Even now Chaves was riding hard for Fort Bayard with the news.

And Dana was not a man to discount plain facts. He knew that, as sure as he was alive at the moment, the mark of Victorio had fallen like a dark cloud over the thin strip of civilization in the morning shadows of the Mogollons.

6

AN OVERSIZE HORSESHOE

FIVE MILES NORTH of the Big Dry, Troop A came upon a lone Navajo Indian. He sat by the side of the road, as still and quiet as a statue. His horse stood a few yards away.

He wore deerskin trousers, sandals, and cotton shirt. His black braids fell glistening and long from a worn felt hat that was pointed to a peak. A huge Indian, small-eyed, big-boned, and absolutely expressionless of face, he seemed at once both fierce and peaceful. Dana sized him up, all the while thinking there were good Indians and bad Indians, the Navajo no exception.

This Navajo simply stared at him, through him, minus concern. When Dana asked a question, he lazily pointed to his horse and then his own foot. The roan was apparently lame.

As troopers fell out of line and sat nursing blistered feet, Dana said:

"Who are you, Navajo?"

For answer the redman, not once drawing in his fixed gaze, fished a greasy neckcord from under his shirt and held out a tag for Dana to read. On it was printed:

Navajo called Indian Joe. Scout for Queeny Mining Co. A. T. McQueen Mines, Luke Mason, Mgr.

Dana looked at the horse, then back at the steady eyes of Indian Joe. The look in them caused his glance to fall on the knife in the other's belt. Somehow, it was a menacing blade; in the sunlight it glittered. He raised his voice to the farrier and said:

"See to his horse."

Indian Joe looked on as the farrier sergeant lifted the pony's feet one by one to his apron and examined them for cuts, breaks, and bruises. The left front foot seemed to puzzle the farrier; he placed a new shoe over the old one, lowered the foot, and tried it over the right front shoe, then the two hind shoes.

"Well, I'll be damned!" he said.

"We haven't got all day, Sergeant," Dana said, with the usual crispness of voice.

"But this is odd, sir. One shoe is bigger than the others."

Dana started. The massacre of Gutache Mesa, the reason behind this costly march north, was so much in his mind that he became instantly alert to the tale the southbound wagoner told yesterday—*Trucks of only one pony about the wagon, and it wore shoes, which Apache ponies didn't. And* THE LEFT FRONT SHOE WAS LARGER THAN THE OTHERS.

Quick suspicion almost got the better of Dana. He did not dare look at Indian Joe then. Instead, he adjusted his campaign hat impatiently and said, with apparent disgust:

"Must have been shod at Fort Bayard. Leave it alone, Sergeant."

He ordered the column to attention, then gave the signal for route step. Indian Joe walked at the head with his horse, as though content with the company he was in.

Dana drew Reeder to the rear of the wagons and said: "Send a couple of sharp-eyed troopers back to the Dry, Sergeant. Tell them to look for the track of a big left horseshoe at the scene of last night's ambush."

The town of Bacon appeared on the river like a strip of heaven to the last man of Troop A. Sprawled in the shade of cottonwoods, nondescript marquees carried a word to rival the finest watering places in the world: SALOON. And the "Loo-tenant," though a martinet, was also a man, and the odds were long that he'd say, "Wash the dry down your throats, men." The inevitable would follow, the limit per man, the duration of time. Then, sure enough, he said it; not word for word, though it was all the same.

38

The citizens of the town watched Troop A move in. To them the grimy dust-caked troopers constituted a formidable outfit. Heavy cannon and a brass band, bunting flying and guidons out in the wind, could have added little to the glory of the troop. This was in a word reinforcements. Victorio would think twice before starting trouble now. But Bacon did not know that three dead troopers lay in the paymaster's ambulance.

Lieutenant Dana stood inside the Frontier Saloon. Oblivious to the crowd, he took time out to beat the dust out of his trousers with gauntlets before looking at the bottle and glass Jason Muench set out for him. Drinking one, he favored the citizens with a hard, grim face. The squint was still with him, and it lent his eyes a sharpness like anger, in keeping with the working ridges of his jaw muscles. He gulped a second glassful, wondering if the fellow Sack, in the Adjutant General's favor, was looking at him, if and when he would make himself known. He said at last:

"Night attack on the Dry. Lost three men."

That broke the silence. Talk buzzed and questions fell fast. No one asked whether Apaches had done it; that was a settled fact. So was the future. War was declared, by deed, the Apache way. Silence gathered in spots, and faces looked at nothing, eyes unfocused before snapping alert again. Dana read men's faces, saw cattle and farms and homes and children uppermost in their minds. Peace had fled the Valley. The picture of things to come was one these men didn't wish to see. But they were staring it squarely in the face.

Dana felt a surge of anger. Though he was convinced that it wasn't an Apache war, he knew the Apaches would fight it. And so would he and his men. The war threat was close and real. It melted into his discovery of a large left horseshoe and ran on to the tag worn by the Navajo, who was a scout for McQueen. And doubt of McQueen, and questions he could not answer, ran in and out of his mind.

He poured again and looked into the small glass. He didn't know McQueen. He had never been to Queeny. How honest or grasping the rich mine-owner was he had no way of knowing. But the silent Navajo had been close enough to the Big Dry.

Dana glanced up quickly. A man with a red mustache was saying in low, guarded tones: "Between you and me, Lieutenant, I can't get used to somethin' I ain't heard of before. 'Paches don't strike at night."

As Dana's look sharpened, the little man said:

"My name's Sack. Got a room at the back of this buildin'. Shade's always down."

Dana looked at him for some time. "Know the Adjutant General's name, Mr. Sack?" Sack spoke it, and Dana said, "I'll be in your room in half an hour."

Having shed the mantle of highwayman, Young slept in the open near the river. For a long time he had lain quietly, looking up at the icy stars as he tried to reconcile all that had gone before to all that lay ahead. The future misted over. Only the stars were real. Next to them Bonnie shone with lucid brightness. He knew she was all she seemed to be, that she had been stirred by him as he had been by her.

And with the dawn she popped up in his mind, straight up from out of his heart, to completely obscure her father and his own driving purpose. But with daylight and cold water in his eyes, he was once again himself, a man bent on a single mission.

That had been yesterday, which he spent riding around the country, getting used to it, wasting a day. And today he felt useless. He was getting nowhere.

When Troop A limped in that afternoon, he joined the gathering crowd near the Frontier Saloon, more concerned with his own problems than he cared to admit. For all his trouble and risk, he had accomplished little if anything. To make matters worse, he had no definite plan in mind. With nothing to go on, he continued to put off a visit to the mining town of Queeny.

He was about to turn away from the sorry-looking troopers when a face arrested his attention. He peered closer at the lieutenant in command.

"It's Dana, all right," he said to himself.

Shades of the past, the recent Mescalero campaign. It stirred unpleasant memories of Captain Corday's unmilitary tactics; of Chief White Moon's strategy that came from the opposite direction which he, Young West, had predicted to the hot-headed Lieutenant Dana. And Dana blamed him.

That was the story. And Dana was entering the saloon.

Young looked out over the sunbaked mesa toward Queeny Canyon, then across the road at the livery barn. And still something nagged at him, told him to wait, that his last hope was up at Queeny. He must not wind up in defeat there. Slowly he walked to the back of the saloon building and on to Sack's room.

With no answer to his knock, he tried the door and found

40

it unlocked. He walked in and sat down. A little later Sack came in.

"Glad you're here, Kid," Sack said. "Seems we struck on somethin' to think about."

Then he launched into the story of the night attack on Troop A. Young listened, aware of what would follow. War was inevitable.

"Three dead troopers," Sack said thoughtfully.

"Did you say the attack came at night?" Young asked.

"Right. Five arrows. The mark of Victorio. Mason said Victorio spent five years on a reservation."

"Who is Mason?" Young asked.

"McQueen' manager and future son-in-law."

"Son-in-law!" Young masked his surprise quickly. "Well, Mason's right. Victorio spent exactly five years at San Carlos."

Sack was studying him closely as he added, "But I never heard of an Apache night attack."

"Nor did I, Kid." Sack leaned forward and pointed a nger at Young. "I'm in need of a man who can mix judgment with guts and powder smoke. You'll do."

"Much obliged, but I've got a job of my own, Mr. Sack. You know what it is."

"Sure. I know. But in servin' me you might be servin' your own self, Kid."

Young smiled dubiously and said, "I'm all ears."

"All right. Listen. This Lieutenant Botts up at Gutache Mesa said there was only one set of horseshoe marks after the prospectors were killed. No provisions or horses stolen. Does that sound like Apaches?"

"No."

"Then who done it? Let's look a little deeper. The prospectors who was killed left a sack of heavy ore with Jason Muench, the barman here. Burns and Chalmers had hit a bonanza up on Pueblo Creek."

"Go on," Young said, without interest.

"So did your old man strike pay dirt. He was done in, wasn't he? Similar, ain't it"

Young's glance sharpened. "It is at that," he admitted. "But what are you getting at?"

"Just addin' up two and two. The Gutache murders look phony. So does the attack on Troop A last night. Somebody around here wants that Pueblo claim, and war to boot."

"Who would want war?" Young scoffed.

"I don't know. But I've heard of white men profitin' by Injun wars. So have you. But what I'm gettin' around to is this

41

—whoever it might be could be the same one who got your old man so he could claim his mine."

"I'm beginning to see it," Young said. "And Indian trouble will scare off a stampede up to Pueblo Creek. Maybe it's working that way now."

"Well, I ain't heard of nobody rushin' up there to stake a claim."

Young got up, walked to the window, and stood lost in thought for some time. He said: "It's something to go on, which is more than I expected. But where do I come in? What's this job you have in mind for me?"

"We'll have a visitor pretty soon, Kid. I'll tell you then."

"Visitor? Who?"

"Lieutenant Dana of Troop A," Sack said.

Young whirled. "Dana!" he exclaimed. "What the devil!" Before Sack could reply, Young said: "So you're in cahoots with General Bent, are you? Well, the Army can fight its own wars. I stood my hitch as a scout and got a kick in the pants for my trouble. And who wants to fight a war for the politicians who won't keep their word to the Indians? This won't be the last Apache war. Not by a——"

"Hold it, son," Sack grinned. "Ain't you forgettin' it's not a 'Pache war now? It's a war for private gain, I'm thinkin'. And so was you thinkin' the same a minute ago."

This silenced Young, and Sack went on:

"You have no choice, Kid. You're sucked into this mess, same as everybody else. Only you've got more reason to see it through than the next man. Your old man's mine will still be there when this scrap ends."

"Maybe so," Young replied, moving to the door. "But I don't work for or with a hot-headed officer like Dana. Not again."

A light rap on the door sounded. Young stopped still and waited. With Sack's "Come in," Dana stepped inside. He had not quite closed the door when his eyes thinned to mere slits. Sack saw the hostile glance between him and Young.

"Meet Young West, Lieutenant Dana."

Dana's eyes slid off Young. He sat down and said crisply, "We've met."

"So it seems." Sack looked from one to the other and raised his brows.

"Down to business," Dana said. "And alone." His look pierced Young.

"He stays, Lieutenant. He's in it." He proceeded to tell Young's story, which failed to impress Dana, then said in summation, "So if I'm right in thinkin' it ain't a 'Pache war under the surface, the Sacaton Kid can uncover more than you and me put together."

Next he said: "What's on your mind, Lieutenant?"

"A healthy dislike for incompetent scouts, particularly this one. He cost me the lives of several good troopers."

Young got up and said cooly, "That's a lie."

Dana stood, bristling. "Now is it, West? In the Army we rely on scouts. You brought in the wrong information and you know it."

"It was the right information when I reached you. The trouble with you boys who learned war at the Academy is that you never give the Apache credit for having any brains. You're no exception, Dana."

"Call me an Academy officer, will you—me, with ten years of it out here?"

"That's what you act like," Young said. "And you're a liar to boot."

Sack saw two strong men evenly matched and both seeing red. Dana was in a belligerent mood and he showed it, while Young masked his anger with that brand of cool indifference Sack admired.

"Now, boys," Sack said, stepping between them, "this ain't no time for a grudge fight. Personal differences can wait. The Adjutant General sent me up here to do a job, and he told General Bent to trot an officer up here who would back me all the way. How about it, Lieutenant?"

Young showed surprise at what Sack revealed. Dana moved reluctantly to his chair and said: "Very well, Mr. Sack, since you put it that way my hands are tied. But," he added, glowering at Young, "my time will come."

"Sure," Sack smiled humoringly. "But right now I'm mighty interested in that *Apache* night attack."

As Dana launched into the story, his anger seemed to cool, though a strong and permanent resentment at the invisible evil forces at work broke through his words. Young and Sack saw the chill gather in his eyes and every line of his face and they felt the frustration of helplessness in the vengeance-minded soldier. He talked on through the silent shower of arrows and to the morning sadness hanging over his troop. Then he was telling about the lone Indian and the lame horse.

Sack sat taut as the story came to an end with:

"The left front shoe was larger than the others."

Young stared at him and said, "Who was the Indian?"

"The tag read: 'Navajo called Indian Joe. Scout for Queeny Mining Company. A. T. McQueen Mines. Luke Mason, Manager."

"McQueen!" Young said, looking at Sack. "It's beginning to unfold."

Sack was pacing back and forth. "Well, I'll be damned," he said again and again. Stopping still, he added, "And more'n one person said Mason looked sort of half absent without his Injun."

"I haven't met Mason," Young said.

Sack examined Young closely, speculation in his glance. "No. You ain't, Kid. But you will. In fact, that's the first thing you should do. That's your job for the present, if you want it."

"I'll take it."

Sack nodded, then said, "I reckon you'd better saunter up to Queeny—as the Sacaton Kid."

Dana left them, saying he would return shortly. He joined them a little later, just as Young was about to take his leave, and said: "The troopers I sent back to the scene of ambush rode in a few minutes ago. The only tracks off the road were made by a pony with a big shoe on the left front foot."

7

AT THE GREEN PALACE

As YOUNG RODE into the log-and-tent town of Queeny at around seven that evening, Charlie Wyatt rapped on the door of the finest room in the Green Palace Hotel.

Luke Mason opened the door and said: "So it's you, Charlie. About time you got here."

"Me? I tried for two days to find you, Luke. Here and at the mine."

"I've been up on the north road looking around. Went as far as Pueblo Creek."

Charlie sat down on the side of the bed and watched Luke select a tie before the mirror.

"You got a lot of trust in the 'Paches," he said. "I ain't."

Luke chuckled. "I'm not afraid of them. Not yet, Charlie." Then he looked at the A-T foreman and said, "Did A. T. catch the stage robber?"

"That's what I come up to tell you. The damn fool brought the payroll sack in. Got through the trap we set. He was talkin' to Bonnie when we got back."

"So you got him," Luke said absently.

"No, we didn't. Seems he's totin' a grudge. Told A. T. who he was. Said he was John Hammond West's boy. On the prod for whoever killed his old man."

Mason's hands remained still at his collar as he looked into his own eyes in the mirror. Slowly he turned his face on Wyatt.

"West's boy, you say?"

His intent look held as the other said:

"That's right. And he told A. T. off. Right in front of the new deputy, Sack."

"Just what did he say to A. T.?"

"Sort of accused him of killin' his father. And when A. T. said everybody knew 'Paches got West, the Kid up and says Victorio was on reservation at the time."

Mason looked sharply at Wyatt and said: "Do you mean to tell me A. T. and Sack let him get away with robbery?"

Wyatt told all that happened at the ranch and inside the Frontier Saloon, ending with: "And that's how it turned out, Luke. The Kid wouldn't draw and Sack stood up for him."

"The two-bit robber!" Luke said. "And Sack needs to learn who's running this country." He turned to the mirror again, saying, "So he's John Hammond West's boy." Shrugging it off, he frowned upon Wyatt. "But what's all this to me, Charlie?"

"Throws suspicion on A. T., don't it?"

"Did A. T. send you here?"

"No."

"Spill it, Charlie," Luke said crisply.

"That's about all there is," Wyatt said.

Luke turned around. His face was minus all geniality.

"Listen to me, Charlie. You didn't come up here just to tell me this. You're where you are because I put you there. I've cut you in on a few good deals because I wanted to stay in the dark. But you sit here with all sorts of innuendoes—insinuations that is, Charlie—playing loose on your tongue. Hinting that A. T. and I got rid of West, aren't you?"

Wyatt felt the icy light in Luke's eyes, the threat and politeness in his voice, but most of all the power of Luke Mason which did not emanate from any talent for gunplay or physical force, things that he could understand. Luke had a way about him, a polished, reserved, authoritative way that added up to prestige. Charlie knew he wasn't a man to cross. He said:

"No, I ain't thinkin' that. Instead I was facin' a fact, that there might be some who probably will think it and talk it up."

45

"You're quite right," Luke said.

There was some excitement out in the street. At the window Luke and Charlie listened to the rise and fall of voices as the stage driver gave an account of what had happened to Troop A on the Dry. Three men dead; five arrows; the mark of Victorio.

Charlie shook his head and thought of what it meant. He said grimly:

"Looks like war."

"And short profits," Luke growled. "Miners quitting and the mine shut down. Hell to pay. It's about time we organized our own militia."

"Militia?" Wyatt looked puzzled.

"Sure. Unless we can offer the miners some protection against the Apaches there won't be one left in Queeny this time tomorrow."

Wyatt agreed. He remained at the window, looking absently down on the street. Indian Joe entered the room and Wyatt turned to see him lifting hands and stabbing at air with fingers. Luke nodded and talked sign language with him.

Then Wyatt saw something in the street. He said: "Come here, Luke, and see who's ridin' into town." Luke followed Wyatt's pointing finger. "That's him," Wyatt said. "West's boy, the Sacaton Kid."

Luke studied the rider closely. In a quiet voice, he said:

"Charlie, we'll make it a point to be nice to this Sacaton Kid. I might find a place for him in McQueen's Militia. Now go on down and buy him a drink. I'll be down a little later."

Wyatt departed, and Luke, with white vest and dark coat to enhance his good looks, glanced at the mirror again and walked out of the room. Indian Joe followed him down the hall and stood outside the door Luke was about to enter.

As Beulah Orbon opened the door, Luke smiled down at her, liking all he saw, dark red hair and green dress and large blue eyes now looking soberly up at him. Her face was interesting, intelligent, and decisive; and always alive, as though she carried invitation in it. A large mouth and a few freckles on her nose did nothing to detract from her strange beauty.

"You heard about it, Luke?" she said.

He knew she was talking about Troop A out of Fort Mangus, though another presence in the room caused him to ignore her question. He looked at the man standing at her window—

Big Dan Turrentine.

He was a man of huge figure. Nothing flabby about him; rather, he suggested a manly strength likely to draw admiring

46

eyes of both men and women. His face was heavy though genial, his eyes penetrating and soft, and a man knew at once that he was a peaceful sort.

Luke mastered his quiet fears and dislike of the man, smiled and answered Beulah, "Yes, I've heard." Then he addressed Turrentine:

"You should have sold out to me last week, Dan."

Turrentine looked at the glowing tip of his cigar and said:

"Reckon you're right, Luke. War and mining don't mix well." Turning away from the window, he favored Luke with a speculative glance. "Does the offer still stand?"

"I'll give you exactly half of what I would have paid you yesterday, Dan."

What Luke said next seemed amiable, his ease and tone of voice and expression were all friendly enough, though something hidden in the cadence of his reply annulled the impression:

"We've played cat and mouse a long time, Dan."

Beulah felt the sudden tension. Luke saw the thinning intensity come into her eyes.

"Meaning?" Turrentine spoke up.

"Nothing. Just looking at your ore and ours. We're digging poor rock, both of us. But we'll buy you out if you care to sell."

"I'll think it over, Luke."

"I mean now, right now," Luke said. Before Turrentine could cover his surprise, Luke was saying: "Beulah, your color is green. It goes with your hair."

"Thanks, Luke." She placed a glass in his hand, ahead of Big Dan. "We'll drink to—just what?" She laughed.

"To an end of this Indian trouble," Big Dan said, drawing from Luke a pleasant chuckle and—

"For once we're in accord, Dan."

They drank. Conversation seemed drawn to the unprecedented Apache night attack on the troopers. Turrentine said it sounded "fishy," and Luke said three dead men sounded real to him. Both men looked at Beulah, glanced at their watches, and talked on. Turrentine arose at last and said he had to leave. He was at the door when Luke drew his full attention.

"Plan to keep your mine going, Dan?"

"How? This war will scare the last miner out of Queeny in a hurry."

"So you'll close down. Better sell tonight, Dan. We'll buy, provided you agree to leave Queeny for good."

Big Dan's brow furrowed and his eyes sharpened quickly.

"Some day I'm going to get enough of your threats, Mason. They're coming too damn often of late."

"No offense, Dan. None at all."

"That's what you say. Yet you keep it up. I wonder if it's mining competition in your head, Luke. Or something else."

He looked at Beulah, opened the door, then closed it again slowly, and said:

"You're supposed to marry Bonnie McQueen, aren't you? Are you planning to knock at this door after that?"

Luke said, with utterly unperturbed face, "I am."

A wave of color pushed up under Beulah's skin and she glanced at Luke as though he were proposing an open affair. And suddenly she knew that he was doing just that, forcing her to look cheap before Big Dan.

"I'm warning you not to enter this door after you're married. Remember that, Luke Mason."

With that, he left them. Luke continued to stare at the door.

"You made me look bad. Why?" Beulah said.

"Didn't mean to. But it's a showdown."

"And it might as well be right now," she said, with purpose up. "I won't see you after you're married."

"I'm not giving you up, Beulah."

"Oh, yes, you are! And right now." She was on her feet, her blue eyes afire, her lips trembling into a tight line.

Luke was up also. He held her at arm's length and looked at her, laughed in light mockery, then baffled her with a soft glance.

He said placatingly: "Quiet now and listen to me." His way stilled her and he went on: "I'm not marrying Bonnie McQueen, I'm marrying all A. T. owns. It's you I want, Beulah. And there's no mine trouble be.ween Dan and me. Never was. It's you. But it's over a mine if trouble comes."

She stared at him, seeing a calculating man with prodigious ambitions and the soft tread of a cat. He would get what he wanted, regardless. As she looked at him, she felt a loathing, a strange fascination, both working in and out, both vying for supremacy. She could go a long way with him, but Dan offered marriage.

Luke was gentle with her. He drew her to him as though she were a precious figurine; returned her look of panic and indecision with a gold glance that was as soft as it was firm, as trusting as it was dominating.

Her mouth was tight when he touched it with his, though he loosened it with a flood of fierceness. The waves of warmth and hunger, a moment before all his, engulfed her as a

48

cresting wave rolls over a beach. They were one in that long moment. And when she broke from him, there was less decision, though a struggling desire for it, in her face.

"You're not giving me up!" he said.

A glance at her expression was enough for Luke to know he had won again.

8

McQUEEN'S MILITIA

YOUNG WENT STRAIGHT to the dining hall of the Green Palace Hotel, missing Charlie Wyatt, who waited in the Silver Bell Saloon. In Young's mind was a picture of the town on both sides of a mountain creek closed in by towering canyon walls. Tents with feeble candlelight inside turning them yellow; horses, and the smell of dung mixing with cooked onions and the sour smells wafted out of the log saloons; one long street, as narrow as two passing wagons which moved on, one with McQUEEN on its sides, another one with BIG BEULAH; dogs and children playing in the street, and drunk miners staggering by with songs and oaths declaring their various stages of abandon; a house on the hill with saucy girls calling down to anyone who would listen; a square adobe house, more rows of tents, and a woman's shriek and oath and a man's growling words; then suddenly a long two-storied building and men who dressed better; gamblers, and a larger saloon, the Silver Bell, with freshly painted green batwing doors. The sign over the building read:

GREEN PALACE HOTEL

A gem in a pigsty, thought Young.

The food was good enough, and served in generous quantities, to lessen the gouge of steep prices. He was finishing up a dish of apple cobbler when his attention was arrested by the entrance of a tall man and a large Indian. The former sat down at one of the tables and the latter, a Navajo, stood with arms folded in the corner a yard or two away. Quite impressive, though rather unusual, Young observed, thinking that he had come upon Luke Mason and the Queeny scout sooner than he had expected.

From the crowded stools at the counter, a man said, "See Luke's shadow got back." Young looked at Mason, who

49

could not have been deaf to the bass voice, and saw that he paid no attention to the remark.

Old Loco Tom was saying, "I jest got in myself." Young saw Mason look up with interest, then glance at his food again as a few of the men began asking how much solid silver Tom had fetched in this trip.

"I ain't sayin'," Loco Tom replied. "This town's gettin' too durned inquisitive."

Young was paying for his food when a voice from the back of the room arrested him, "Aren't you the Sacaton Kid?"

Every face turned, as did Young's, to the table. Luke Mason was standing, a friendly expression on his face. Then Mason said, so everyone could hear his carefully spoken words:

"Mr. West, join me. I was just thinking about our need for a man like you. We're organizing McQueen's Militia—to protect the families and mines here."

He came up, introduced himself, and stuck out his hand. Young took it and, urged forward by a friendly arm and enthusiastic greeting, was soon seated across from Mason, who was saying:

"Thanks for an opportune visit, Mr. West. By risking your embarrassment in front of all those miners, I may stop a stampede out of Queeny. The miners will get the word around fast."

"About the Sacaton Kid?" Young asked, pretending to be on guard.

"The name won't hurt any, though I spoke of the militia. By the time we visit the Silver Bell Saloon, we'll have twenty volunteers."

"Militia," Young pondered aloud. "Not a bad idea at that, Mr. Mason." Before the other could reply, Young said, "How did you know me?"

"News gets around fast, particularly if a man is handy with a six-gun. I know a lot about you, West, how you took the payroll sack to A. T. and told him what brought you up here. Sorry it had to be the death of your father years ago, but I'm glad you're here just the same."

Young kept his eyes off the Indian who was staring through him with a show of unconcern. He said:

"I didn't come up here to join a militia, but I'm foot-loose. I reckon I can look around on the side—for the man who killed my father."

"Now that's the way to look at it. If I can be of any help in tracing the murderer, call on me."

Young studied the face before him without seeming to do

50

so. He wasn't ready to place an estimate on Mason yet, despite his easy grace on one side and his Navajo on the other. He had met men like Mason, suave, helpful, and sly, and men like him who were sincere. He said, testing McQueen's manager:

"Think 'Paches got Troop A's men last night, Mr. Mason?"

"Frankly, I never heard of an Apache night attack. Did you?"

"No. And I've scouted for the Army. Even slept within a hundred yards of a Mescalero war party without any fear."

"Are you employed by the Army now?"

When Young laughed and said, "Hell, no," Mason said seriously: "Night attack or not, West, trouble is in the air. It's war now. And somebody must take the lead if the mines are to stay open."

"If you're trying to convince me of something, forget it. Just what do you want me to do? And how much does it pay?"

A light of suspicion flickered across Mason's eyes; for a mere fraction of a second it was there, just long enough for Young to assess this man: he would not cheat you at poker, for poker was a pastime to this natural-born card-player; he would not offend you in any way, he was too busy trying in his clever unnoticeable manner to draw you out while he held his reserve and made you admire him for those qualities he possessed; but all the time he was thinking for himself, of only himself, using you; and when you found him out it would be too late. All this Young felt even as he thought of Bonnie as this man's wife within a few weeks. However, he had no proof that Mason was that kind of man, any more than he had positive proof that the Navajo was responsible for the Gutache Mesa and Big Dry murders.

"You can head the militia, West. And I'll pay your price," Mason was saying.

"Who gives me orders?"

"I do," Luke said, without hesitance.

This straightforward reply was more to Young's liking. "All right. But no private wars are included. Is that understood?" Then he named a stiff price.

A little later, Luke introduced the Sacaton Kid to the patrons of the Silver Bell. He bought drinks for the house, stood up and extolled the gun speed and eye of the Sacaton Kid who had robbed McQueen, and then had the guts to return the payroll sack. The word of the militia had swept the town, and Luke played it up, saying that he and the mineowners would pay out their own money to protect the families of the miners who cared to stay and work; that the owners owed the town protection; that the Sacaton Kid would see that Queeny remained a safe place to live and work in. He held them with his infectious enthusiasm.

Young was not blind to the value of Luke's persuasion, which was nothing short of timely artistry likely to forestall a wholesale evacuation of the town.

All the while Indian Joe stood apart from Luke, silent and dumb to all appearances. Young thought he seemed watchful.

"No private wars, no uncalled-for acts of violence. Any man wanting to join up will swear to obey the rules the Sacaton Kid lays down. The militia will organize, then disband. Men will go to work, all of you, tomorrow as you did today. The bell on the Green Palace roof is the signal to rush to arms. All right, who wants to join up?"

A big miner stepped before Luke and said, "I swear."

It was as simple as that. Within an hour forty men knew what was required of them: a rifle, a pistol, and obedience to orders. When it was all over, Luke bought another round of drinks and held up his hand for silence.

"Now," he said, "I'm appointing a second in command. If anything happens to the Sacaton Kid, you'll take orders from Charlie Wyatt."

Young looked at Charlie Wyatt, who grinned up from a chair directly in front of the gaunt and silent Navajo.

9

THE SON OF VICTORIO

ALL WAS QUIET in the Mogollons. No Indian signs were reported during the two days following the birth of McQueen's Militia. The miners went about their work as usual, and the bell atop the Green Palace remained as quiet as before. Lieutenant Dana and Sack rode up to Gutache Mesa for a talk with Lieutenant Botts. Word of the militia reached them there. Sack smiled when he heard that Mason was behind it and that Young was in command.

A. T. McQueen didn't smile when he heard that the militia bearing his name had for its head the Sacaton Kid. Wondering what the hell ailed Luke, he got into the saddle and rode for Queeny.

As usual, his visit was an occasion. Along the crowded

street of the canyon town people pointed him out and said, "There goes McQueen." His horse walked with a man of note on its back, and the route from the first tent to the Green Palace was nothing short of a march of triumph. McQueen enjoyed it, and on this afternoon it softened him up more than he knew.

Along the street he heard: "If it wasn't for McQueen, there wouldn't be nobody here today," and, "McQueen took the bull by the horns to protect us with his militia." As a consequence, he forgave Luke for sponsoring the idea long before he walked through the batwings of the Silver Bell. But his mind was set on another score: the Sacaton Kid had to go.

The first man he met inside the saloon was Big Dan Turrentine. They shook hands, causing a wealth of speculation regarding rumors of bad blood between them. However, fresh opinion formed quickly, that the two had put aside their differences for the duration of Indian trouble.

"Congratulations," Dan said. "It was the first sensible move Luke has made in weeks, thanks to you. I was ready to close up, A. T."

"The hell you say!" A. T. laughed. "Well, you won't have to now. What's it costing you—your share of this protection?"

"More than what's fair," Dan replied, making a grimace. "But I'll go along since it's your idea."

"Seriously, Dan," McQueen said, in a low voice, "what's come between you and Luke?"

"You really want to know? Dan stared deep into his competitor's eyes. With McQueen's nod of assent, he said, "Suppose you ask Luke."

McQueen went on to the mine. He sat in an ore car and rode the nine hundred feet inside the tunnel to the left fork. He got down and stood by the track examining the rock that came out of the fork while waiting for Luke. Under the lanterns his face took on a dark look. The croppings from the left fork, now a thousand or more feet in, wouldn't assay one hundred dollars per ton. The right fork had shown from three hundred to fifteen hundred dollars to the ton. And yet Luke was continuing to feel out the mountain, letting the right fork alone.

Looking up, he saw Luke; and he asked why the poor ore was worked and the rich vein neglected.

"Why, A. T.," Luke grinned, "I thought you knew. I closed up the lode so our ore will look poor. The word gets around, you know."

"But why? We own the hill."

"Not all of it—yet."

53

"You mean Big Dan's claim?"

Luke nodded. "Which is heading straight for our right fork. I'm hoping that the sorry ore we're mining now will influence Dan to angle off from us."

"I see it now. Sure. And once he does that, he's digging himself bankrupt, eh? McQueen grinned.

"And we'll get the whole hill for little or nothing."

"Damned if you don't beat all, Luke." His hand fell on the other's shoulder, and he said: "I hope you don't get so all-fired busy you'll forget your wedding. Bonnie might not like that."

Both laughed. Then McQueen said: "What's really come between you and Big Dan?"

Luke didn't look at him at once. When he did, the searching glance he sent behind McQueen's eyes, for any knowledge of the affair with Beulah Orbon, was well masked. He could see through A. T. now, as in the past, and what he saw was merely curiosity. He said:

"Gold. Isn't it enough?"

"I don't want any trouble, Luke."

"I'm not asking for it either."

McQueen lifted his brows and eyed Luke. "No? What about putting the Sacaton Kid in charge of the militia I didn't know about?"

"Oh, that?" Luke chuckled once, then again. He sobered quickly and said: "The militia was a necessity. Else we wouldn't have miners until the scare was over. I——"

"I know that, and I've got to hand it to you for thinking fast, Luke. But why the devil did you hire that damn upstart?"

"For two reasons. First, he carries gun weight since the stage robbery. Next, he talked up to you, I hear, spoke a few threats, and made it look as though you might have put his father out of the way. So I decided to put him in his place—by hiring him. Forces him to back down to all appearances."

McQueen was rubbing his jaw with open palm, darting dubious glances at Luke. "Maybe so," he said.

"Stick around, A. T. You'll have a few people shake your hand for your generosity. It isn't every man who's big enough to hand a good job to an upstart that tells him off."

"I hadn't thought of that. No. I hadn't thought of it. But what if trouble does start, Luke?"

"Trouble? Hell, A. T., you couldn't drag the Apaches anywhere near this town."

Both men laughed until the thick rock walls bounced the

54

sounds of hilarity back and forth through the long tunnels of Queeny Mine.

Not a quarter-mile above the town, an Apache slid off the back of a slaty roan mare and gathered up rocks into a triangular pile. He placed a twig on top, pointed it toward the mining town, and leaped upon his horse again.

He was not an ordinary Apache. He wore no rag of red flannel about his head. One bright red eagle feather stuck up out of a white sash at his forehead. Leather and silver bands were on his arms, and about his neck he wore an amulet of buckskin and turquoise. His hair was greased with marrow from the antelope's bones until it gleamed in the sunlight. He was straight and tall and his apron was of deerskin. He wore no boots or robes, and his body was the color of the deep orange crags at sunset.

He was One Eagle, son of Victorio.

He picked a way down the canyon until his eyes traced a path up the sheer walls. Once more he built an Indian post-office and pointed the twig to the west. Next he rimmed out, like a fly up the narrow trail where a slip meant death. But One Eagle knew his way here, even in the dark of night; as well as he knew the habits of the deer and turkey, the cat and the bear; as he knew the location of the juniper berry, the acorn, mesquite bean, and piñon nuts which were roasted for winter.

Few were the mysteries in One Eagle's head. The elements and the spirits of night had been explained to him in his youth, though they continued to puzzle him. The four seasons, from Ghost Face to Red-Brown Earth, were accepted by him because he had seen them come and go. The yucca gave soap and the greasewood brush a tonic, and colors were in the life that grew out of the ground and in the precious earth itself, which, like the sky, remained vast and puzzling.

But predominating among mysteries was the paleface, White Eyes, who was friendly and unfriendly; who gave with one hand and grasped with the other; who spoke promises out of one face and denied them with another; who was something to fear, respect, and hate. And hate was easy with the Apache, whose name meant enemy.

Now on the rim, One Eagle worked on west toward the mesa where charred wagon wheels lay. His mission was one for no other brave of the Apaches, since only he of them all understood the language of White Eyes. As a child he had visited the white trading post and listened. Those were the days of few white men, and peace. Since then war and reservations and doubt and famine had heightened the puzzle of White Eyes.

The sun hung low over the distant range when he espied the strange hogans of the white warriors who dressed in blue. He rode on, and when the tents on the mesa were close, he attached a strip of ragged white cloth to a stick and waved it. A sign of truce. The camp of the white man turned out and he was soon looking at a flag like the one he carried, wondering at the magic of a piece of pale cloth.

Lieutenant Botts invited One Eagle into his tent. He was wishing he knew more about the ways of the Apache, and he was also wishing that Dana were here. But he did his best, though with a certain embarrassment. The Apache was saying:

"Me One Eagle. Son of Victorio, Chief of the Apache Nation."

Lieutenant Botts, for all his ignorance of Indians and Indian warfare, showed a trace of excitement. An important Apache, as this one surely was, stirred his ambitions. The devils of career tempted him; they said treachery wasn't treachery, but an expedient; that this was war. But Botts was as timidly indecisive as he was small and round-faced and pink-complexioned—his size had given him a complex in the Academy, and he had therefore turned scholarly, had graduated with book honors into his lieutenancy. He said:

"I am listening, One Eagle."

"White Eyes has seen his men die. In this moon. My father has sad face. He sends vedettes out. They see many soldiers moving into the land of the Apache. Has great Victorio turned his back on his word?"

Lieutenant Botts blinked his eyes rapidly as he considered this.

"Three soldiers have died by Apache arrows. Two prospectors were thonged to the wheels of their wagon and burning arrows were sent into their bodies. Apache arrows."

"Not Apache arrows, Chief of White Warriors. I have been sent here to tell you this."

The Lieutenant smiled dubiously. He was thinking that the Indian lied, not knowing that the word of an Apache was never broken; that by lying One Eagle had violated the truce. Therefore, treachery on his part was no longer existant. He said:

"You must speak your message to another white chief."

"I have spoken. I go."

Lieutenant Botts thought better of it. Seeing only the son of the dreaded Victorio in his hands, he called the corporal and ordered One Eagle bound. His order was carried out with quick dispatch. Botts, with six cavalrymen and the prisoner, struck out for Bacon in the waning daylight.

Night had fallen like a thick blanket when they reached the junction of the Queeny-Bacon road and met a Troop A courier bound for the Gutache Mesa camp. The message which Botts read by matchlight was from Captain Corday, who had just arrived in Bacon with Troop B. It was brief: "Meet me in Queeny at nine this evening."

It was an order. Lieutenant Botts looked at his watch, saw that it was eight o'clock, and decided the jog down to Bacon was useless. So he did what any young officer might have done, he turned his little detail up the road to Queeny without any thought whatever of the excitement an important Apache prisoner might evoke in an already war-alerted town. But he soon learned.

Lanterns on tent poles and campfires in the town lit up the passing detail. One Eagle's feather and bronze body quickly arrested attention. A grizzled old man ran alongside the Indian a few steps before yelling forth:

"I gads, sure as they call me Loco Tom, it's Victorio's boy! One Eagle!"

The news ran ahead of Lieutenant Botts who was by now aware of his error. Somewhat startled by the forming crowd and the surge of miners at the rear, he rode on, his sole item of hope the respect due his uniform. And this served him as he moved to the Green Palace Hotel, where he dismounted and marched his six men inside with the prisoner.

Looking out at the crowd which kept growing, he felt a small wave of triumph. It inflated his ego as nothing else had ever done, since this was the first time in his life that he had actually done anything out of routine. He smiled and felt larger in size, felt a certain luminous glow shining out of his blue tunic. Big men of the West, to whom he had felt inferior until a minute ago, were filing past him, shaking his hand. Then it suddenly dawned on him that he had captured this Apache devil; that he was actually a hero.

He accepted a drink a cowboy handed him, and he saw no reason why his men shouldn't wash down the dust of Gutache Mesa. After all, the enemy was securely bound; and the Army was not only in charge here, the Army was inviolate. With visions of the two bars he might soon be wearing, and deservedly, he relaxed the guard.

One Eagle said nothing. He felt the uselessness of talk and confined his thoughts to the sustaining pleasures of hate and vengeance.

Upstairs, Charlie Wyatt ran toward Indian Joe at Beulah's door and shouted through the partition, "Luke! I've got to see you!"

Luke appeared and listened. After a moment of silence, he said, "You know the way to the roof, Charlie."

"What about the Sacaton Kid?"

"Just ring the bell," Luke said.

The loud peal of the bell reached beyond the mines, up into the lonely canyons, and down the road to Bacon. Apache scouts straightened, listened, and detected alarm in the tones. The tent town heard and all motion ceased. The crowd before the Green Palace felt its vibrations against eardrums. Lieutenant Botts, with drink in hand, started, and asked about it. The answer was drowned by the noise about him. Outside the hotel, men looked at one another, a few exchanging nods and grins, and broke out of the crowd. They returned soon with rifles and pistols. They waited, all eyes scanning the hotel and street for the appointed leader, the Sacaton Kid.

Moving along at a casual trot, Young, Lieutenant Dana, Captain Corday, and Sack were riding toward Queeny. Dana was saying to Corday:

"The big horseshoe left its print on Gutache Mesa and on the Dry. Five men were lost, sir. And not by Apaches."

"That is all very well, Lieutenant. But you forget the threat of the Apache. It is constant. This side issue isn't. So we'll remember that we were attacked. That, as you know, is reason for a campaign."

"And a damned unjust one," Dana said.

"How was that, Mr. Dana?" Corday sounded crisp.

"Nothing—Sir."

Corday remained silent for a moment.

"West," he said, "this militia of yours should serve to protect the towns while I give chase to the enemy. The more I think of it, the more it appeals to me."

Young said, "But Lieutenant Dana——"

Corday interrupted with a laugh. "Is a hot-head."

Sack said: "Captain, I suggest we look into this Injun Joe business. War is one thing I'll vote to put off any old time."

"Mr. Sack, your attitude is worthy of praise, to be sure. The General would not go against that. But I must inform you again that General Bent and the staff at Fort Bayard are in accord in this matter. The Apache has attacked. And his threat must be wiped out of the Territory of New Mexico. And I'm here to do just that."

Dana was thinking, "Hail Napoleon!" And Young was saying to himself, "He's a damned fool."

Only Sack spoke out with firm conviction:

"Captain, I'm here by the order of the Adjutant General of this territory. And I'm advisin' you to hold off for a while. For your own good."

He stopped short. Young's horse was reined in, as was Dana's. From the north the faint sound of a bell was heard. Then it sounded clearer, louder, a clarion call to action.

Young heard the iron notes of trouble falling over the land. He thought of Luke Mason and Indian Joe and Charlie Wyatt even as he racked his mind for the reason behind the bell. Then he spurred the flanks of his pony and leaned forward in the saddle toward Queeny.

10

"NO ACTS OF VIOLENCE"

LUKE MASON took in the scene at a glance: Victorio's son sat in a corner, a stoic look on his face; one trooper stood guard, his rifle against the wall; miners, cowboys, prospectors, gamblers, and hangers-on filled the doorway, jostling one another for a glimpse at the enemy.

Luke's mind was turning fast from this angle to that even as he made his way to Lieutenant Botts. The bell continued to ring, and he was wondering if Charlie Wyatt planned to make a night of it on the roof. Then suddenly it stopped.

The Army was in Luke's way here. It nettled him at first; until he looked outside. Smiling, he defined a mob as a band of law-abiding citizens with stampede in their heads; as an excuse for violence. All this one needed was a spark.

He turned his charming side to the Lieutenant, who, upon learning that he was Luke Mason, beamed under suave compliments.

"This should hasten your promotion, Lieutenant. And you may count on me to speak for you in the right places. But this mob here. The people don't love Apaches, Lieutenant."

Taking hold of Botts's arm, he walked toward the door. The crowd made way for him. At the hitching rack he called for silence. With the full attention of the crowd upon him, he said: "Take it easy, boys. The Army has the situation under control. Remember, now, you boys of McQueen's Militia, I said there would be no uncalled-for acts of violence." Then he said, looking over the crowd, "Where's the Sacaton Kid?"

His speech over, his innocence of anything that might follow established by his appeal for restraint, he entered the hotel and met Charlie Wyatt.

In a low voice, he said: "The Sacaton Kid isn't here. Take over. Stir them up, but protest all the time against a lynching."

As Wyatt grinned and looked at One Eagle, Luke added: "Burns and Chalmers are dead. Burned with Apache arrows, Charlie, one arrow for each year Victorio spent on a reservation. Think about it. Let it work on them. In the meantime, West may show up. I want him to get the blame if anything happens."

Wyatt walked into the crowd outside, like a dose of poison. Though not as subtle as Luke, he talked of burning arrows and screaming prospectors in one breath and the inadvisability of a lynching in the other. It was like a careless match meeting pine needles in a dry water run. Men talked to other men and these talked to others, on and on until they were saying that Charlie Wyatt headed the militia, that he talked up vengeance. The militiamen soon found themselves in a crowd all their own, a little distance from the main body of citizens, Wyatt in the middle, hard-pressed for a decision.

"Wait a minute," he said. "I can't stop you if you want to go ahead with it. The damned 'Pache deserves it. But there ain't to be no violence."

It was settled then. The Indian was theirs. And Wyatt was speaking of the Army, and sending a man to determine the size of the guard, and listening to the report that came back:

"Hell, there ain't nobody guardin'! Luke's got the troopers in the Silver Bell!"

"All right," Wyatt said. "I can't stop you from wantin' to get even with a murderin' Indian."

McQueen's Militia was of one mind, and moving. Men made a way for the law of Queeny and watched with excitement the march toward the door of the Green Palace. There was purpose in the eyes of these men.

Beulah Orbon had never seen a lynching party, but she knew this was one. As frightening sensations ran through her, she felt the power of men out of control. They were but a few steps from the door of her hotel when she called for Luke and stepped into their path.

"Not in my place, boys," she said.

"All right, Beulah," one miner said. "We'll take the 'Pache outside."

She stood still in uncertainty, scarcely seeing the rider who slipped out of the saddle of a rearing horse and elbowed his way through the militia. He was suddenly at her side and raising his voice to the crowd. Someone yelled, "The Sacaton Kid!" and she turned her face on him.

Young was well ahead of Sack and Captain Corday, though Dana was close behind. The bound Indian inside had drawn Young's eye. It told a story in a flash: the Apache was an important one; the militia wanted his blood, and was about to get it. He felt the weight of their violence and he was shouting, trying to shock them into their senses when he saw Charlie Wyatt urging the men on.

And on they came. Beulah was pushed aside and, before Young could back up and draw his gun, they poured in like stampeding cattle. He was carried along with the wave, neither on his feet nor on the floor. Then they were stepping on him, their deafening yells and shuffling feet drowning his yells.

Something struck him on the head. When he came to, he was astride a strange horse and a miner was holding him erect. They were not moving, and no one paid the slightest attention. Shaking his head in an effort to bring the scene into focus, he knew before he saw the object that arrested all attention what was being done or had been done.

But nothing was clear. Shouts or a memory of them rang in his ears and his head hurt. His fingers touched a spot above his left ear. It was wet and sticky. Someone had struck him down with a pistol butt. The rush of the militia in the hotel returned to his memory, as did the face of Charlie Wyatt.

He could see now.

A huge bonfire lit up the night. Pines and rocks were animated in their own uplifting shadows. And stretching the end of a rope, a grotesque figure kicked spasmodically. Then only the flames danced, and silver bands on still arms, and greased hair, out of which one feather protruded, lent any motion to the lifeless body of One Eagle, son of Victorio.

Young could not remove his eyes from the body. Sick to the bottom of his belly, he wanted to vomit. Silence was heavy, prolonged, and alive, as though Apache ghosts filled the night with wailing sounds beyond the reach of human ears; as though the mob, its lust diminishing, were seeking to shake off its surfeit and return to the same world of men. And One Eagle was no more. Young continued to stare at all that was left of him, wondering as he did so if the departed spirit of the son were now rushing straight up into the Mogollons for a last powwow with the living Victorio.

Someone coughed. The spell was broken. Then a man bent double and groaned. A laugh followed.

And Young asked a question, aloud: "What am I doing here?"

The answer came from the miner who held him up. "Hell, you led us, Kid!"

It came as a shock and served to clear his brain instantly. He saw it all now, though it was something he did not wish to believe; he saw Wyatt, and he felt the suave prodding tongue of Luke Mason behind the foreman. But to the citizens of Queeny and the Army, the Sacaton Kid headed the lynching party. He had ridden out with the militia. He was with it now.

A little distance away were Lieutenant Dana, Sack, Captain Corday, and another officer whom he did not know. Then he searched the militia for the face of Wyatt.

Wyatt wasn't there.

A sickening sense of failure swept over him. The look in Dana's eyes was sharp and contemptuous, and full upon him. And away in the distance he felt he was seeing the hurt and permanent judgment in the face of Bonnie McQueen. And Sack! The omission of any definite expression there seemed worse than total accusation.

A slow fury gathered in him. He knew what he must do. All argument against it was struck down. All fury cooled and one purpose dominated him.

Without another glance at the corpse, he turned the horse and walked it toward the lights of Queeny, toward Sack and Dana, who sat the saddle among others blocking his way. Militiamen fell in behind him, some on foot, some mounted. This was what they had been told to do, he realized. He was the leader, and he felt the mockery of it.

Dana's horse walked out to intercept him. He kept going, though Dana caught the reins and gave them a twist about the saddle horn. Then he took a gauntlet from under his arm and struck Young full in the face with it, saying:

"That's what I think of you and your militia, West. Cowards and traitors, all of you."

Young felt the sting of the gauntlet less than the words. A blind anger leaped high in him, then died away to nothing; all in a split second. Dana was right, and there was not so much as a spark of retaliation left in him.

"Why don't you do something about it?" Dana was saying. "You or the whole of your damned murdering crowd!"

Young sat still. He said nothing.

There was in Young's face that unmistakable calm that Sack defined as a dangerous quality. Dana felt it, thought it oddly out of place here one second and deserving of fresh estimates the next.

Young left Dana. As he rode slowly toward the Green Palace, his mind churned with review of everything that had happened, from cause to effect, from Sack's and Dana's shattered hopes for peace to the puzzle behind Mason's desire for war. Nothing made sense, not even the maze of facts which forecast trouble without end.

But something else was gnawing at Young. Everything pointed away from the ambush of his father. All signs said, "That way, not this way," as though somebody were going to a lot of trouble to hide everything from him. The militia was a farce; therefore, Mason and McQueen were frauds. They were trying to cover a personal war with a real war. What's more, they were getting away with it. And to top it off, Luke Mason had cleverly placed all blame for the hanging of One Eagle on the son of John Hammond West.

"Why?" he said silently. "Why, if he and McQueen didn't get my father?"

But the proof wasn't in his hands. He regretted this, since he knew that he could not complete the work he planned for this night—he could not force Luke Mason to shoot it out with him.

Men along the street were shouting and cheering his return at the head of McQueen's Militia. Hanging an Apache was the quickest route to popularity. The ovation sickened him, forced a tight silence in him. Then he was thinking again, asking another useless question: Why had the Army allowed this outrage? Mouthing an oath, he worked the horse through to the hitching rack outside the Green Palace.

The crowd in the small lobby overflowed into the Silver Bell Saloon. Young made his way past outstretched hands, refusing to shake with any man, feeling that even one handclasp would make him as guilty as he appeared to be. Smoke and liquor fumes filled the saloon as he searched for Mason and Wyatt. They were nowhere about, and he wormed on through to the lobby again, in time to see Sack, Dana, Corday, and the Lieutenant he didn't know coming through the door.

He was inquiring of the whereabouts of Mason and Wyatt when Sack came up and handed him a surprise: showing his badge, Sack said:

"You're under arrest, Kid." His voice carried and silenced the babble of voices.

"What for?" Young asked.

"The Injun belonged to the Army. Your militia took him by force. A serious offense, Kid."

Sack continued: "The Injun was One Eagle, son of Victorio. He rode into Lieutenant Bott's camp up at Gutache Mesa with a flag of truce. He was sent by Victorio with a message—which was that the prospectors and Army soldiers killed wasn't done by Apache arrows. Victorio wanted peace. Think he will now?"

Young's glance fell on Botts. "Why weren't you guarding him, Lieutenant?" he asked. Botts's face was red and embarrassed. "Why would an Army officer bring a lone Apache here, in the first place?" Young went on. "Should have known what would happen in an Indian-scared town."

He saw the flicker of approval in Dana's eyes ice over in defense of the Service; he saw Sack's brows arch up in agreement; and Corday's superior smile. What he didn't see was Beulah Orbon moving to his side. She drew his glance when she said:

"The Sacaton Kid is right about the Army. He's also blameless. I know."

She told Sack of Young's arrival in the face of the storming militia, of his futile appeal to the men.

"Don't sound reasonable, miss," Sack said. "He went to the hangin', didn't he?"

"Unconscious," Beulah said. "I saw the gun butt come down on his head. And I know who did it."

"Beulah!" The voice from the door behind her was commanding. Luke Mason walked to her side and took her arm. "Come now," he said gently. "You've had enough to upset any woman."

"Wait," Sack said. "Who done it, miss?"

"Charlie Wyatt," she said before Luke could stop her.

"I'll vouch for Charlie," Luke said quickly. "He was not present at the hanging. He was with me. And there are a dozen men who'll guarantee it, the same as there are ten times that many who heard my stump speech before the outrage—I warned them against any acts of violence."

Beulah's bewildered look swept from Luke's face to the crowd, who was voicing support of his statements.

She said, "But I saw Charlie in the mob just before they took One Eagle."

"And I seen him," said Loco Tom. A man giggled and asked if he'd bet his secret silver mine on it. "Hell, yes," came the reply. "I seen Charlie."

"So did I," a large man said. "I'm Dan Turrentine, Mr. Sack."

From out of the door to the hallway Charlie Wyatt walked with anger and excitement in his face. He stood level with Big Dan and said, "If you say I was at the hangin', you're a damn liar."

A heavy stillness enveloped the room. Big Dan tensed and Luke's nails dug into the skin of Beulah's arm. Indian Joe moved closer to Luke, and Wyatt backed slowly, his hands hanging threateningly above his guns.

The quiet was broken by Young, who said:

"Wyatt, I saw you in the mob nagging the men on. Why don't you call me a liar?"

"I will, you damned coward! You're a liar!"

The crowd thinned in a hurry. Luke shoved Beulah aside and cried, "Make room! Somebody's liable to get shot!" Sack said there would be no shooting, though he didn't sound convincing. With men lining two walls, Wyatt with his back to the third and Young standing near the fourth, the stage was set for a show the West excelled in.

Young said: "Wyatt, you've asked for trouble ever since we met. You're liable to get it. All I want is the truth from you. Cards face up, Wyatt."

There was no reply, and Young appealed to him again. "Why not admit it? You're a grown man."

Wyatt's feet were pushed apart and his barrel-back and shoulders were hunched forward. He looked tense and darkly forbidding with elbows back, and hands inches above his guns.

In sharp contrast, Young stood at ease, both thumbs hanging from his belt, no excitement breaking the set calm of his face. But for all his outward relaxation, he was watching Wyatt with those gray eyes, watching for the flicker of warning that he knew would precede by an instant the road of Wyatt's guns.

And then he saw it, and he was all impulse, and action.

Wyatt's hands fell to his guns and jerked them up with incredible speed. He seemed confident that he held an advantage, for a twisted smile went with his draw. It was anticipated triumph and the glory that would come to the man who cut a notch in fame over the dead body of the Sacaton Kid.

With that warning signal from Wyatt's eyes, Young's right hand slid to his gun with the rapidity of a flash of lightning. There was no interim, no split-second of waiting for a blaze of fire, the gun in Young's hand exploded as he jerked it backward.

Only one shot sounded. Wyatt's guns remained silent as

his knees slowly buckled under him and a wild look of disbelief wiped the smile off his face. Then he pitched forward on his face and lay still.

No silence could have been more complete, no stillness more pronounced. All motion seemed frozen but for the lifting layers of gun smoke about Young. Out of a single roar, this, and every eye fixed on Charlie Wyatt, and every eye next on the Sacaton Kid, who stood as before, quiet in pose with thumbs hanging from his belt. Then he spoke, and his voice, low and easy, sounded loud and harsh:

"He was somebody's tool. Too bad he had to pay for the man who still has his coming."

Slowly his eyes lifted from Wyatt and swept the faces in the room, on around until they rested on Luke Mason. The look that passed between them was stripped of all pretense.

Young backed out of the door into the night.

The rent healed. Men spoke to one another again, talked louder and milled about. Only Sack stood as though still lost in the spell, his unfocused gaze on Luke Mason, who turned to his Navajo and made a sign; insignificant, perhaps, though the fingers of one hand curled up like the talons of an eagle. Five fingers. That was all.

As Indian Joe disappeared through the doorway, Luke approached Sack and the Army officers with grave face and voice.

"And I'm the man who said there would be no acts of violence."

11

CALM AND CONFUSION

YOUNG TOOK an off-trail route to Bacon that night. His sense of danger sharp, he paused at the mouth of the canyon in a screen of oak brush and waited out a long quarter-hour.

The stars were thick and low and bright. The memory of the night was dark. An innocent man had stretched on a rope, and another had paid the price of treachery conceived by a more cunning man, which proved that life was cheap in the schemes of men.

He was thinking Sack's decision to arrest him, and wondering if Corday had forced it, when the sound of muffled hoofs reached his ears. He soothed his horse and clamped fingers in the animal's nostril to forestall a whinny. The quiet fall of hoofs drew nearer until the moving bulk of horse and rider took on distinguishing shape.

The rider was Indian Joe.

The picture he made in the starlit night was to Young an invitation to destroy this savage machine. Reason asserted itself, however, telling him that the Navajo constituted the sole hope of evidence against Mason and McQueen. Alive, he might be of use to Sack and the Army in pointing to the killers; dead, he would be the lost clue. But it wasn't easy to think of a killer's eventual worth to a cause at a time when his own life was at stake.

He knew the Navajo was innately a bloodhound. Indians of the open West sensed the presence of a human being. He was not at all surprised when Indian Joe stopped his horse within a dozen yards of him and felt out the surroundings with more than human ears. Then the Indian sent his pony into a lazy trot. He was soon swallowed up by the night.

Young rode on cautiously, very alert in himself, picking his way to the river and following the stream all the way to Bacon. The lights of the Frontier Saloon winked out as he unsaddled his horse at the livery barn. Searching out every shape in the night, he made a circuitous approach to the back of the saloon.

Sack's window gave to his applied strength and he was soon inside, lying in the dark with boots on, listening. A few minutes later he was asleep.

The sun was an hour high and flooding the sky with light behind the Mogollon peaks when he sat up in bed with a start. A key grated in the lock and Sack entered, stood still for a long moment of appraisal, then said:

"A good place for you to be, Kid."

Young relaxed, got up and worked the sleep out of his arms and legs. "I could eat a mule," he said, watching Sack shed his coat. He said no more until the host poured water out of the pitcher into the big bowl and washed his face and hands.

"The town was sort of keyed up after you left last night." He looked at Young. "Did the Injun trail you?"

Young nodded.

Sack told of Mason's talon-like sign to the Navajo, and Young related the incident of the night.

"So you had the gumption not to shoot him, Kid. Good."

"Why don't you arrest that killer?" Young said.

"What for? So Mason can swear he had nothin' to do with it; so he could be warned of all we know and laugh at us?

Captain Corday thinks you and Dana and me fools already."

"What about my arrest?"

"It sticks, Kid. Corday is all rules, and Dana don't love you enough to take the gauntlet out of your face. I was right proud when you took his glove calm like."

He eyed Young closely and went on:

"Damned if you didn't shoot fancy! Queeny drunk up barrels of rotgut last night talkin' about it. Wyatt didn't find his trigger. But," he said circumspectly, "that makes the McQueen crowd all the more scared of you. And all the more set on doin' you in."

He sat down and drew a long breath.

"Kid, I never took my eyes and ears off Mason last night. He's got the town in his hands, and he's shrewd like a fox. We're up against brains there. At about midnight he got up and went upstairs. He was in Beulah Orbon's room. She is the woman who accused Wyatt. I heard him eatin' her out for namin' Wyatt. She stood up to him and said Turrentine wasn't schemin' like him, which set him off. Seems there's bad blood between Turrentine and Mason. Over Beulah. Then Mason got nice and she broke down."

Young was on his feet. "Hell, he's supposed to marry Bonnie McQueen!"

"Yeah! I never thought of that." After a lapse of seconds, Sack said: "Well, I left for the mine—me and Dana—just tryin' to add up two and a question mark into four. My badge got me a miner's light and we went inside. McQueen and Mason are minin' poor assay right along. Odd, I thought, when there's heavy gold ore in the right tunnel. So we went back to the hotel and visited this Turrentine, who sketched a map of the hill and his tunnel and the mouth of McQueen's tunnel. Seems McQueen and Mason are blind-foxin' Big Dan. Then we talked some more and added up the two we had with another two. We got four—which is that a private war is on. For a mine and Beulah. Big Dan admitted it."

"I think it's bigger than that," Young said.

"Could be," Sack meditated aloud. "But that's all that shows up to now."

"That and two dead prospectors. But try to put your finger on it." Young stared at the walls. "Like proving they killed my father for the mine."

"Right."

"So you play your hand out," Young said, bitterness in his voice, "deuces or aces. I'm holding the low pair against McQueen and Mason."

"Don't forget the Army. You're under arrest, you know.

In fact, Kid, you haven't paired against *three* aces." He added, "But you can draw cards."

"What do you mean?"

"I want you to go along with Corday, Dana, and me. I finally convinced Corday that he had to make a bid for peace for policy's sake. I think the hangin' of One Eagle made him see it. So we're callin' on Victorio soon."

"You're a day late."

"There's always hope," Sack said.

"You're a day late."

"If we can stave off a 'Pache war, we'll nip the McQueen-Mason scheme at the bud. Then, with Turrentine on our side, and a close eye on the Navajo by all of us, we'll dig out the stink—maybe all the way back to your father's death."

Young studied Sack's face, considering all he had said.

"It sounds good. Too bad the Army blundered yesterday. One Eagle was Apache, so I say again, you're a day late."

Bonnie called her father twice before removing her apron and stepping outside. The early morning flush of color in her face was explained by the savory odor of ham steaks and coffee. Seeing several cowboys knotted in conversation at the horse corral, she walked toward them. They scattered strangely before she reached the gate.

"What ails everyone?" she called out. "The bunkhouse usually empties in to hurry up biscuits. They're ready and cooling."

The pokes came to the table, a little quiet and secretive, she thought. Their silence was unprecedented, as was their lack of appetite. Something was wrong. With her father absent and unaccounted for, she looked them over one by one and spoke to the last one on the end.

"Percy Southworth, look at me." He obeyed. "Now what's come over you boys?"

"I say, Miss Bonnie, it's deucedly odd. Jolly well embarrassing, don't you know."

"You English!" she exclaimed, before facing a cowboy named Jones. "Bugs, spill it, and right now."

"Sure. Only I thought A. T. would be back by now. Luke sent for him in the night. Well—Charlie Wyatt was shot last night, Miss Bonnie."

"Shot!" A bowl of redeye gravy slipped out of her hands. She paid no attention. "Who shot him?"

A hushed silence and out of it Jones said, "The Sacaton Kid."

The pokes were looking at her. They saw all color go out

69

of her face and her lips part in disbelief and meet again. She stared at them with wide unseeing eyes and said almost inaudibly, "The Sacaton Kid!" Slowly the natural push of pink showed in her face. She was herself again, though not without courage on her part.

"Was the Kid hurt?" she asked calmly.

"Don't know."

She was standing, then walking toward the door.

"Bugs, saddle my horse," she said. Turning about, she looked them over carefully. "So you boys are thinking of going after the Sacaton Kid. Well, you're not. Understand?"

"Why, Miss Bonnie, we ain't happy to know Charlie was done in. We——"

"You'll draw your last pay from this outfit if you leave the ranch today," she said, as businesslike as a man.

Glances were exchanged among them before Percy said: "I say there, Miss Bonnie. I'm having about the soundest time in years. And I'll lay a bob or two that these chaps are in accord. Eh, what?"

"He means he likes it here," Jones said. "I reckon I do too. I'll stick, if just to learn Percy how to talk understandin' like."

"Noble of you, Bugs," she said. "What about the rest of you?"

One by one they voiced one excuse or the other for remaining on. Satisfied, she left them.

She was riding toward Bacon and her face was hot, and all the rebellion in her seemed to push up into her cheeks and eyes. There was decisiveness in her movements as she dropped out of the saddle before the Frontier Saloon. She walked through the batwings and asked for Joe Sack.

Luke Mason was there. He stared in amazement, and came to her and said, "Bonnie, this is no place for a lady."

As his hand caught her arm and he urged her toward the door, she said crisply: "Turn me loose, Luke. A lady is a lady anywhere if she's one at all."

He smiled placatingly. "All right Bonnie. But come on outside."

She walked out with him.

On the porch, he said: "I don't want my future wife talked about." Then he eyed her critically. "What made you go inside?"

"You heard me ask for Mr. Sack, Luke. I'm mad as hell. About Charlie Wyatt getting shot."

"So that's it." He felt easier now, though he turned a grave face upon her. "He didn't stand a chance against the professional gunman. Too bad you took his side that night," he put exploringly. "A. T. might have demanded his just dues."

"I did what I thought was right," she replied quickly. "Was he shot up also?"

"No. Too bad, since he led the mob that hung One Eagle. War is inevitable now."

"War? One Eagle? What are you talking about, Luke?"

He was glad to oblige her with his version of the entire affair. Had he spoken one word in defense of Young, she might have honestly resented it; but he painted with total malice. Knowing that Young was not all Luke imputed him to be, she was suddenly defending him in silence.

"There'll be war, all right," he was saying. "Can't be otherwise. You know what that means; anything can happen. I'll be hard-pressed to keep the mine going, Bonnie. May have to take up a gun myself. In the face of it, everything considered, I'd like for us to get married right away."

He was convincingly in earnest, and she was placing him alongside Young, his good looks, success, and stability against a gunman's future. Putting down everything vaguely stirring and then strongly at work in her, she resolved to put wisdom of the head over a woman's uncertain heart.

She said: "Whenever you say, Luke."

He had not anticipated so quick a victory, but what Luke thought and showed were usually at variance.

"Sunday night all right?" he said.

"This is Thursday. Charlie will be buried in the ranch cemetery tomorrow. I don't like the timing."

Her very thoughts put to words stirred up another for close examination: Wyatt had been fond of and faithful to Luke, and his death did nothing at all to Luke. She suspected and saw for a fleeting moment a cold callousness in him. She told herself that he was covering his grief.

"Bonnie, Charlie wouldn't mind."

"No. He wouldn't mind," she said slowly. "All right, Luke."

She looked up at him, at the man she had promised to marry, expecting a little show of elation, the expression of it. Her face invited him. She waited, saw him nod his head and smile, felt the touch of his hand to her shoulder, then the brush of his lips—at her forehead!—and heard him say, "I'll see you Sunday."

He was getting on his horse. He was on the Queeny road, Indian Joe trailing after him. She watched Luke, wondering what there was in a man who failed to respond to the invitation in his future bride's face.

When she took her eyes off him, Sack was walking toward her. She looked at him for a moment without seeing him in her mind. His greeting and, "When's the weddin', Miss Bonnie?" caused her to remember suddenly why she was in Bacon.

"Oh," she said, a little bewildered, "Sunday night, Mr. Sack." He started and a furrow creased his brow, which puzzled her. Under the sharp scrutiny of his eyes, she said, "What's wrong with Sunday?"

"Nothin'. Nothin'. I was thinkin' about other things, I reckon. The trouble up at Queeny last night, and the threat of Injun warfare."

"And the murderer you and I let slip through our fingers that night?"

"Murderer, you say? Somebody has been workin' on you, Miss Bonnie. The Kid shot Wyatt in self-defense. Fair and square."

"My, but you're a lenient officer of the law! I hear he led a mob and hanged an Indian first."

"Seems your mind is made up. So I don't reckon I'll try to change it none. But if you ever want the truth of it—say between now and Sunday night——" He broke off suddenly, then said, "I talk too damned much."

Curious, she said, "Go on. Say it."

"All right, I will. Go see Miss Beulah Orbon. She runs the Green Palace Hotel at Queeny."

"Thanks," she smiled. "I may do just that. In the meantime, if you see the Sacaton Kid, tell him to remember I said I'd fight against him as hard as I fought for him. I'm beginning now."

"Tell him yourself," came the curt reply. "He's not a quarter-hour at slow trot up Gutache Mesa road."

Her glance sharpened. Mounting her pony, she said, with contempt, "A fine deputy you are."

She left him standing still, shaking his head over the eternal puzzle of woman. He could not possibly know that she was turning over in her mind his "Say between now and Sunday night," trying to reconcile his pointed mention of her wedding to the "truth" of the Queeny affair. A discerning woman, she wasn't long in realizing that he was warning her about Luke. It wasn't easily dismissed, not with Luke's passive kiss as fresh in memory as the uncompromising guilt he prescribed to the Sacaton Kid.

She was of a sudden very anxious to hear what Beulah

72

Orbon had to say, and the story Young had to tell. She drew her pony up and looked north, then a little east of north to the canyon that swallowed the town. Her decision made, she struck out upriver.

A midday haze lay on the mountains before she sighted a lone rider topping a knoll. He dropped out of sight for a long time. A blistering sun stood at zenith, furring distances, while heavy clouds gathered over the Mogollons at her right. Rain was a promise, a mockery. The smells were dry and dusty. The clouds were, like an old rancher had said, "Probably empties coming back."

In the shimmering distance, high on the range that spurred eastward out of Arizona Territory, the White Rocks appeared like snow. There, it was said, Victorio kept watch over the Valley. The thought of a white woman's fate at the hands of Apaches sent a shudder through her. She forgot it and rode on at a gallop.

Young was closer and she topped the bald hillock he had ridden down. He was skirting a clump of thorny oak when he turned suddenly in saddle with gun up. He put it away and waited. She walked her pony down, expecting the lecture that men gave women who rode alone out in the cactus stretches. He said nothing of the kind, just looked at her.

Halting a dozen feet from him, she sat out a moment of appraisal and judgment—Luke could not be right all the way; there was too much good behind Young's eyes, a clean pride in his face and a challenge that went beyond any testimony against him, beyond right and wrong. It flooded her with warmth and gladness. But something separated them. He had warned her father. He had begun on Wyatt. This made them enemies.

He sensed the latter and fought off her attraction. But persisting challenge and courage flowed out of her for him to see and feel. Though irritated by her steady show of independence, as well as by the circumstances that placed them on opposite sides, he was unable to deny that she was all he desired in a woman.

She said, her low voice husky but calm:

"You know how to set a stage for a killing, don't you? You're building a reputation for the Sacaton Kid. A professional gunman. It should be easy for you, you're gentle and polite and innocent-looking."

She paused, and he said, "Go on, Bonnie."

The calm and patient reproof in his glance served to work up rage in her.

"I told you what I'd do if you wanted to fight us. You de-

73

stroyed a life that God made. Who's next, Luke, or my father?"

He waited for more. But she had spoken her piece and was staying on just to declare her determination and enmity in silence—this she told herself, while the inner woman waited, hoping for some obscure sign of his innocence and some word from him. He didn't humor her; instead he accused her with a long penetrating glance, which he broke off with lazy suddenness. He turned his horse and, with back to her, made his way around the thorny oak.

Surprised, she stared resentfully. Something inside her kept saying she was stubbornly prolonging a mistake. But she had spoken and her pride wouldn't let her bend.

Furious, at him and herself, she called out:

"If Luke is next, better get him before our wedding Sunday night!"

That drew him up short. He sat erect in the saddle, looking at her. "Don't do it, Bonnie."

He rode away then, and she watched him until he dropped behind a large knoll in the distance. She felt a queer sense of weakness, of being drawn to him, and she turned and rode hard in the other direction in order to keep from running after him.

12

ONE SLIM PEACE HOPE

IT WAS JUST BEFORE the break of dawn next day. Lieutenant Dana's disgust was complete. He looked out into the Indian dawn. He thought this was the last silent dawn of peace between the Apache Nation and the white man. The trumpeter had not yet split the air over Gutache Mesa. The flats were hemmed in by shadows of the night even now, and they talked on in the tongue of night birds and other strange languages that were neither Nature or Apache, or both. In war, one forgot that Nature had a voice. Dawn was God's listening post, God's and the Army's, though it was the latter sitting up to a man with ears trained for the hellish throat rips of savages.

But Dana's thoughts were an evasion.

He was thinking, first, of the mess Lieutenant Botts had made of things; and in the scope of it, Captain Corday wasn't blameless, in that he had been forced by a hanging to do what he should have done before it—strike a bid for peace.

Next, One Eagle had not been removed from the tree until nearly noon. Apaches weren't blind.

Then Sack, who worked strangely, was making a farce out of West's arrest. The Army could not allow the mob incident to go unpunished; for the prestige of the Service, not to mention military laws. Nor would he, in Corday's place, let the damned Navajo run loose when evidence pointed to guilt.

But today, this morning, the all-important bid for peace would be made. The odds were against success. In summation, the reasons for the change of odds were enough to evoke disgust in any man. However, that was the Army, the civilian, which combined proved that everything man meddled in came to ruin. So he put all these things aside and looked at last night, on McQueen's porch . . .

Bonnie was at first listless and distant, a little pale and troubled. He attributed her humor to the loss of their foreman. She warmed gradually into a genial mood and he was telling her about social life at Fort Bayard. Her hand brushed his and sent electric sparks through him. And, startlingly, he knew at last he was in love for the first time in his life. And it tickled his sense of subtle vengeance; too long the Army had been his mistress. However, one bondage was broken by another. He knew this the moment he looked up at Bonnie again.

Damn! He was in love with Bonnie McQueen.

Denied the time for private pursuits, an Army man is jealous of every second. Dana, after long years in the Service, felt the dominating urge to win Bonnie without unnecessary delay. He was here today, somewhere else tomorrow. But experience had taught him a thing or two about women. He resolved instantly to find out where he stood. It was open reconnoiter when he asked if she and Mason were really engaged; and retreat and re-form when he learned they were to be married Sunday night.

A man's honor closed his mouth on all he knew about Luke Mason—his Navajo, and the deception he practiced on Turrentine, and his bid for Beulah Orbon as related by Sack. He got up stiffly, crestfallen and bitter.

He said, "I can't tell you why, but you're making a mistake, Bonnie."

"You're the second man to warn me today."

"Who was the other one—Sack?"

"Young West."

A hard anger took hold of him.

"As much as I despise West, he's right for once. But what right had he to——?" He broke off, and she smiled, as if amused.

Then she was all soberness, asking him about the shooting of Wyatt. Who was to blame? And he was in a humor to tell her Wyatt had forced the gunplay.

She wasn't glad to hear this, then she was.

She said: "Mr. Sack said if I wanted the truth of it I should go see Beulah Orbon."

Amazed, he said quickly, "The truth about what?"

"Why, the gunplay, what else?"

"Nothing. Nothing at all."

"Which means there's something else I should know. About Luke, of course." Then she was examining him closely, a look of sudden suspicion and discovery in her expression. "About Luke and this woman, isn't it?"

He made no reply, and she said: "Thanks a lot, Lieutenant. I'm grateful. More than you know." And her hand fell over his, causing his heart a faster beat.

Then she said something else:

"For I've hurt someone today—badly." She was gazing off into the night. "I thought he murdered Charlie."

He saw it all: for some reason she was marrying Luke Mason when the stars in her eyes were for Young West . . .

But that was last night.

In the slow opening eye of the dawn, Dana stood with hands on hips watching the ragged outline of the peaks. The forces at work in him were hard and grim, half military, half personal, all disgust. Peace or war remained a puzzle, an impersonal thing that somehow was no longer his responsibility. The personal fire would not cool. Bonnie kept it raging, against Young West.

A man walked past him to the highest point of the camp and stared in every direction.

He returned and said: "Morning, Lieutenant. It looks like a fine Apache dawn."

"Is that a prediction, West?"

"Just thinking."

"As a man under arrest or as a scout?"

Young met the brittle glance and said, "Both, maybe."

The trumpeter's brassy notes shattered the morning quiet.

Dana let the call die before saying, "War might be in the prisoner's favor, West."

"I wouldn't be under arrest if the Army knew its way with the Apache."

"Coming from you I don't like it."

"You didn't like it before I said it, Dana. You were damned quick to blame me for the lynching night before last. And you'd rather rot out a career at Fort Mangus than testify in my favor when the time comes. But you'll do it, Lieutenant, even though you're hunting for guilt in me, hunting hard and deep, hoping to find it before I'm up for judgment."

The look between them was strong and unsettling, and silence did nothing to lessen the mounting challenge from one to the other. The presence of Captain Corday and Sack merely repressed spoken disregard, and a long hour in the saddle through, brutal, sawing vegetation of the hills kept the memory of their animosity poignantly fresh. Dana's face seemed as tautly drawn as catgut on a fiddle when Sack said a smoke signal was in order.

Clothed in a somber morning haze the distant White Rocks drew all eyes with hope and doubt and memories in them. A fire was soon going and fed with greasewood. A blanket released heavy smoke. It columned upward. With the proper signals repeated twice during the next hour, peace talk resolved into the uncertainty of waiting. Patience went with hopes and eyes scanning the now sunlit mountains. Sack tamped tobacco into a curved pipe, divided his attention with alternate glances up into blue distances and down to the obscure thing in his hands. Dana stood motionless, his tall figure stamped with a sort of brittle dignity. Corday, long-legged and handsome, was the same dashing officer with the usual touch of mocking humor in his face to reiterate his opinion of this necessary farce. The six cavalrymen seemed more alert, and uneasy.

Young looked them over one by one, wondering in idle detachment at their various reactions to failure. He intercepted a look of open hostility when his glance fell on Dana. The tensions of an open duel stood between them.

Sack said, and there was something final in the tone of his voice, "I reckon I'll fire up my pipe." It might mean anything from failure to renewed patience, but it gave them something to think about. Corday looked at him with curiosity on his rather quiet face, though he wasn't to be goaded into asking a question. Young saw this, and he saw a thread of fear running through the alert troopers.

High on the primitive rocks an eagle flew to his nest. Down at Bacon, in the dropping distance, a six-horse hitch stirred up a cloud of dust. The stage wheeled south as usual.

No visible apprehension there, no disturbance of the morning peace hanging over the Valley. All was quiet, very quiet.

Corday said they had waited long enough.

"They haven't finished their councils," Sack said.

Corday laughed. "You don't mean it!"

Dana turned a sharp arresting glance on his superior, who stiffened under it until Sack intervened with "Reckon I do, Captain Corday." Reprovingly. Then, as if to take the edge off the silence, he said:

"Victorio might be holdin' out against the braves. A big white flag on a pole wouldn't hurt our cause none, Captain."

"Sure," Dana spoke up, his voice crisply bitter. "The kind Lieutenant Botts didn't honor."

"Mr. Dana," Corday said icily, "some things are better left unsaid."

"It's too late for that."

There was in Dana's reply all the stubbornness and inner flame that sent and held him to Fort Mangus.

Corday let the matter drop there. Sack said no more about a white flag, though Corday decided later to raise one. Another hour moved slowly by, and the sun blazed new designs on the White Rocks. Heat waves danced, and beyond the western range a heavy slanting cloud threatened rain over in Arizona Territory.

A new haze over the distant hills drew their attention. It wasn't smoke that rose up between them and the slopes under the White Rocks.

"Dust!" Young exclaimed.

"From ponies without shoes," Sack said.

Corday looked from the trumpeter to Sack, who shook his head negatively, and then up at the white rag that had meant little to one of his lieutenants. "We're only ten strong," he said, trying to estimate the odds that stirred up the dust-cloud.

Dana stared at the man who came out of the Mescalero campaign a hero, and his look asked what had become of the gallant veteran. And Young was thinking that some men didn't learn at all, they merely looked good on the crest of some fortunate deception not of their doing. Just carried along.

The dust hung in the distance instead of coming on toward them. Young knew, as did Sack, Dana, Corday, and the six troopers, that Victorio was now leading his braves toward them at a walk. Single file, in a column that might stretch out to kingdom come. If they were in war regalia, Corday's fears might be justified. But retreat now wasn't conformable to laws of self-respect. These ten men had asked for an audience. And it was here they must remain or forever lose face. It wasn't individual or personal any longer; it was a matter of racial honor.

And every second was a long one. Minutes multiplied. All the quiet of a thousand years surrounded them. The sun baked the mesas and shone on the pine and aspen of the high reaches and the amber and brown of the bald ridges and flats. Over the rolling hills toward the White Rocks it was the same. No dust. No sound. No sign. All the differences among them were sucked up into the ageless vacuum. They were one in waiting it out, one in expectancy.

A horse topped a hillock a quarter-mile off. A redman sat erect and still. Another popped up a little to the west. A dozen more showed on the ridge. Corday's little band was all but surrounded when over the northern line of the highest knoll there appeared the big feathers; not one chieftain but many. The line held, no motion to it, waiting, the united Apache Nation.

The arrow would be broken or sundown smokes would lift red from the highest ridges.

As though time stood still, the Apache and the white man stared at one another for a long time, the former adept at it, the latter covering his impatience by searching for a white flag.

Then, as if to further impress White Eyes, the horde of warriors Victorio had purposely withheld moved up from behind the screening hills. Fifty, one hundred, and another hundred of them, mounted, red ochre gleaming with the colors of ponies and red-flannel headbands. In all the regalia of war; and still no white flag appeared in the Apache ranks.

"We should ride out to meet them," Dana said. "Troopers to horse and parade for fifty yards."

"Of course," Corday replied, looking at Sack and Young.

Mounting, the four walked horses toward the feathered group. Corday gave the order to the troopers. They halted in a line, heads up, shoulders squared, horses still. The gold tassels from the trumpets gleamed like the polished brass. With white flag up and stirring restlessly above them, the token force appeared weak but magnificent.

Corday led the foursome another hundred yards. There he stopped. The Apache should meet him halfway. And four pairs of eyes were still searching the hill for a white flag, and the minds behind those eyes were asking if Victorio was refusing a truce.

Victorio's arm raised slowly. His white horse moved down

the hill at a walk. Only one Apache followed, on foot. The shaman or medicine man.

Dana said: "They've reached a decision. Else the other chieftains would follow." His glasses were up then, and he scanned the hill. "I see Chief White Tail. All hell and no brains. The other big feather is Hochiti—you remember the Pelona Massacre. The others look like Chiricahuas, though that doesn't make sense. All renegades, perhaps."

Sack said: "I know Hochiti. Looks like we've bagged a war."

"We'll soon know. But I see old Short Pony and St. David. They don't want war."

Victorio came on. With head high, looking fearlessly ahead, he was a king in his own right. His soft buckskin robe was white, and on it were markings of the sun and rain. Silver bands on his arms gleamed. On his head two feathers stuck up out of a head sash. His face was streaked with red ochre, intensified by white outlines. The shaman, a fierce-looking Indian with head shaved, and clothed in holy shirt, ran ahead of the chieftain, bowing, prancing, swinging his medicine cord.

"Look!" Dana exclaimed. He was watching another Apache who rode after Victorio. "It's Terribio, his son-in-law."

Terribio, captain and warmonger, was huge and fierce-looking. Reports from San Carlos Reservation defined him as ungovernable. He looked it as he sat on a bay pony, his wide and flat evil face a picture of hate and murder.

The white horse stopped still and Victorio sat atop the trained animal a dozen paces from the white men. He was a medium-sized man with an interesting, intelligent face; deep, rawboned, richly bronzed. His eyes were steady and determined, though a sharpness in them lent him the cold expression of a bird of prey. Yet there was something in the face, or behind his eyes, a hint of the endured pain of kingship. It struck a spark from Young's imagination and, somehow, identified this chieftain as a wise and patient father of his people, certified him as a man who favored war only as a last resort.

Young knew that pressure brought to bear on an Indian chief by his braves was no different from that experienced by a white ruler. In evidence of this, old Short Pony, on the hill, had long ago stepped aside in favor of Victorio, who in his younger days called for war in the council.

Dana knew a little Apache, Corday none. Sack suggested that Young act as translator, to which Corday agreed, saying, "Tell him we wish peace, but are ready for war."

Young advanced. "Greetings, great Chief Victorio. The

White Father wishes to declare his friendship for the Apache. There are those among us who seek a warpath. But they are few and the White Father spits on them."

Corday said, "Did you tell him we're ready for war?"

"No," Young said.

"Then tell him," Corday said crisply.

Dana said, with contempt, "You don't do it that way—sir."

Before Corday could say more than "Mr. Dana!" Sack intervened. And Victorio was talking, saying slowly:

"Many moons I have asked my braves to cool their arrows in the snows of Ghost Face. I have forbidden my braves to steal horses of White Eyes. I have not led war parties into the land of Mexico because it was forbidden by White Eyes. I have not burned fields and houses of White Eyes. But White Eyes sends devils among us with water that is crazier than tiswin, and guns that bark like the dog and spit fire. Devils kill white man with Apache arrows and kill white warriors with Apache arrows. My scouts have seen the dead. And still I ask for peace when other chieftains come in search of a warpath.

"I sent my son One Eagle among you with peace talk. His white flag you spit upon. White Eyes placed my son on tree like antelope hung up to dry.

"There is no peace among us now."

Young translated this, then said, of his own accord: "That is why we seek great Victorio. White Father sends us to say that white men who took life of your son, One Eagle, shall be punished and Victorio's people will be paid in blankets and corn."

Dana interrupted, "Don't say it in English yet, West."

Victorio said, "There is no peace."

"You cannot win," Young said persuasively.

"There is no peace. There is war among us. White man will die the Apache way. White man will see his fields and houses burn. Your squaws will be treated the Apache way. There is war among us."

"It's war," Young said in English.

Victorio said: "Your white flag angers me and my people. Take it with you and go. I will honor it before I spit upon it. And when you are where my eye cannot see you, I will turn my warriors loose to kill you."

So saying, he raised a hand and Terribio drew his bow and sent an arrow through the white flag. Then he turned his horse and rode for the hill. Terribio was last to depart.

It was war. The seriousness of it was in the grave faces of

Sack, Dana, Young, and Corday. Victorio had spoken the end of peace. Dana cursed and Sack looked sad.

Young said aloud: "This will please Mason and McQueen."

Corday said: "When he can no longer see us! That means we're safe only until we get over the first hump."

"Not if we string out so that one of us will always be in sight," Young said.

"I don't trust Apaches, Mr. West," Corday replied.

"I do," Young snapped.

Corday looked at Young, sat out a moment, then headed his column. With arm up pushing south and the cavalry order, "How-ah-o-o," he led the unit at a walk, thus preserving the dignity of the Service. With backs to the waiting Apache horde, the Army was taking its own sweet time.

The file stretched out. First one horse and rider over the hump, then another to take the place. A campaign hat, a yellow neckerchief, a blue tunic, and a horse on and over the second hump before the rear guard went over the first. The third knoll was long and downhill. The tail of the column must take the chance of waiting, of being separated from the main body in order to prolong the promised attack. It was a long way to Gutache Mesa.

Young said: "Go ahead, Lieutenant. I'll wait."

"I don't go in debt to some people. Ahead with you."

It was a crisp order. It was steeped dislike.

They sat still in the saddle glaring at each other, wasting precious time, neither glancing back at the impatient warriors lining the hill-rimmed horizon.

Then they went over the ridge together, both aware of what they would hear in another second. It came, like a cresting wave over the foothills, bloodcurdling and strong, the long, solid Apache throat cry, the thunder of more than two hundred ponies in pursuit.

Far ahead the trumpet, brass in the sun, reached for the ears of the last outpost. Sharp and harsh, it blared forth the call to action, bounced notes off the hills and on over dry arroyos, no hope in its voice now. Nothing but war.

13

THE APACHE WAY

YOUNG AND DANA rode at top speed, rowels to flanks. The yelling came on; arrows sang through the dust, on past them to the ground, too close, a few ricocheting off rocks and flying crazily about. Looking back, Young saw a dozen braves pile over the hump. To the left a pair took to a low runnel in an effort to cut them off when they turned a little east as they must at the foot of the hill.

Young shouted, reining toward the pair. Dana drove in the same direction, drawing pursuit. It seemed incredible that the enemy should reach the gully first. But he did, and he let arrows fly on the run.

Dana shot first and missed. Young's gun came up just as one savage fell to the off-side of his pony. He fired and sent him flying to the ground. As Young rode after the other, the dying Apache sprang up with knife drawn and leaped for Young, a loud primitive yell issuing from his throat, then choked off in his own blood. He was dead before his body touched the ground.

This was the enemy. No fear in him.

Dana picked off the other.

Young felt a tingling up his spine as he leaped the gully and tore through thorny oak. He expected an arrow any moment. He fired on the run, but with effect. One horse fell and tumbled another, and he saw an Apache leap high and stiffen before the trampling hoofs of Indian ponies.

They had not gone another mile when an arrow caught Dana's horse in the neck. The animal reared high, screamed, and ran on a dozen yards before falling and rolling over and over to the rocks of a dry wash. Young saw Dana on his feet, limping, but running fast just the same.

"Not a chance!" Dana yelled when Young cried, "Ride double!"

Dana was on his belly firing uphill when Young slid from the saddle and ran for the deepest cut in the run, calling Dana after him. They were shoulder-deep in it front and rear, the crook of the little gorge protecting them from the north. But the southwest side was open, and the Apache wasn't long in shifting his main attack to this vulnerable spot. And worse, the entire Apache Nation was rushing down for the kill.

"Short on ammunition," Young said, aiming carefully. He fired, and Dana fired, and the circling horses kept a respectful distance.

"You're a damned fool, West. You could've gone on."

"Yeah," Young replied. "I don't know why the hell I didn't."

He turned suddenly and his pistol roared in Dana's ears ahead of a savage yell a few yards away. The Apache's head hung over their breastworks as they blazed away at a dozen rushing ponies. The charge veered off when two fell in the dirt.

"Belly flat!" Dana shouted.

The thunder of hoofs came on, right over them, leaping over, dust and throat rips, arrows flying down, and then one Apache dropping on them, a fanatical light in his eyes, a knife thrashing air and finding Young's arm. One pistol shot and Apache blood trickled across Young's face. They had for company another dead man.

"Close!" Dana said. "Too close." Then he said, "Never thought I'd sell out this cheap." He blew a drop of sweat off his nosetip and looked at Young's arm. "Nasty cut, scout," he said, with contempt.

"Says the Command of Fort Mangus," Young replied, looking at the open gash of his left arm. "But I won't die from blood poisoning," he added, looking at the foe who had drawn off into a silent, inactive circle.

"Victorio," Dana pointed. "Something in the wind. Could be their losses; about eight to none, I'd say."

The conference ended. A lone Indian rode toward them with hand upraised. Within pistol range he halted and spoke his piece. Victorio was offering them surrender. Young talked to Dana, then answered the emissary in Apache.

Both were thinking of honey in nostrils and black ants; of burial up to the neck while they rode ponies down on the head, hoofs clawing and tearing; of fires they stuck a man's feet in; of the rattlesnake death; of even worse things. Surrender! It was worth a laugh even in the face of death.

Neither laughed. The grim weight of the situation bore down stark and real. They should be dead. Victorio's half-hearted attempt reminded them of a cat playing with a mouse. Now the real act was about to begin. It would end the Apache way.

Dana's glance fell on Young, who was saying, "This is it." Something in the slit of his eyes, the curve of his lips, held

Dana's attention. "And I don't know yet who got my father."

A light curse fell from his lips ahead of low words about being caught in a war he wasn't interested in.

Dana was curious. With nothing to do but await the finish, he said, "You think McQueen did it?"

"He and Mason are in cahoots. And Bonnie will marry Mason."

"I don't think so," Dana said.

Then he told him of Bonnie's apparent change of heart, concluding with "She thinks a lot of you."

Young detected regret and bitterness in Dana's voice, enough to surmise what went on in his heart. Pleased with the news about Bonnie, he was also surprised that Dana's heartbeat responded to her.

"Odd, isn't it?" he said, taking in the ring of warriors.

Dana knew what he meant. "Is it?" he retorted.

"Yea"—Young pressed the point—"since we won't ever know which is the better man. Here they come, and Terribio's leading them!"

Victorio seemed in earnest now. His strategy called for a few warriors from the north, south, east, and west in a given rush, another and another wave following, falling from horses to close in and overpower the weak white foe. The action began. Dust rose to the sky amid heathen yells; arrows showered down; bronze waves in thundering charges; shots, screaming horses rearing high; bullets, the last few from the little gorge. Powder smoke choking like the dust and pony hoofs gouging up more of the latter. The howling was closer, upon them.

Then the long blasting file of a trumpet. It went unheard amid the throat howls.

Again the trumpet split the air with its brassy cry. Closer now. The wave fell back from its dead to reform for a last charge. But the bugle talked, and its voice was magically disconcerting to the redman.

Victorio sent one little band into the mouths of Corday's guns, then another, and soon split his forces for retreat in a dozen directions. He knew his strength lay with the gods of geography, in the canyons. His offensive was retreat. Drawing the pursuer on, on into ambush and death. This was the Apache key to victory.

And Captain Corday, hero of the Mescalero campaign, humored the hate he held supreme, flattered the strategy of Victorio by splitting his outnumbered unit into pursuing details!

Young opened his eyes and managed to rise just in time

to hear Dana utter a strangled cry of protest. Wobbly on his legs, his hands clawing slowly into fists, Dana stood there for a long moment. Then he pitched forward on his face.

The blistering sun hung dry over the Indian dead about them. Young, bleeding from several cuts, felt the grime and sweat burning into wounds and scratches. The inside of his mouth dusty, lips parched, the retching stink of sun-hot Apache bodies within reach, all these things kept him on his legs. By sheer force of will he stumbled to Dana and turned him face up.

A mumbled oath told him Dana was alive, though barely over the line. It was difficult to determine where sweat ended and blood began on the black tunic. The silken neckerchief was both red and yellow, though the blood was from the Lieutenant's head. Arms and chest and left leg bled from minor cuts. The Command of Fort Mangus might live. Young studied the sullen face, thinking Dana was all man.

Corday returned shortly. The surgeon worked over Dana, who came around before the troops returned.

Lieutenant Botts's detail trotted in last. Young saw Dana jump to his feet when Botts said, "Captain Corday, I regret to report Trooper Benson's capture by the Apaches."

Young said, "Alive?" Botts nodded his head solemnly, causing Young to turn his back. Anger surged in him, battering down his reserve.

No control left in him, he whirled and said to Corday:

"You know what happens to captives. You know Benson's fate. Why did you take the chance of chasing the Indians, Captain?"

"Mr. West, I don't answer to you." He added, with a smile of superiority, "Fortunately."

"You're right when you say fortunately, Corday. I'd break you. Sure as hell I'd break you down from the man you think you are to the one you really are."

Before Corday could reply, Young turned his back and struck out for Gutache Mesa on foot. Something inside him advised that he would never make it under his own power, though the will to do it was tempered by fury and contempt. He trudged on, falling, getting up, and doing it all over again. His arm bled more freely with the exertion, and when the surgeon rode up, he was in no humor to refuse assistance.

When he opened his eyes in the surgeon's tent, the first man he saw was Corday. Cursing, he rolled over and asked for a drink of whisky.

Just before dawn next morning, the horses on the picket

line became nervous. The sentry alerted the Captain and the camp came to life. In the heavy stillness and quiet, ears sharpened and men fingered rifles with strange affection. The color of night was lead and the stars seemed to pale with the approach of mock dawn. Sentries were contacted in silence. All was well. Then the camp emulated the hills and mountains and mesas, waited like them for the mobile universe to shake off the night.

A sentry heard it first, a moaning sound that ruffled his nerve ends. He passed the word, heard it again, and waited. He knew this land. The dawn belonged to the Apache.

A crawling detail came up silently, moved on its belly out to the sound, guns held above the rocks in the snake advance. No chip of metal against rock, that was the order.

The day was taking on shape when the detail returned with the body. It was lowered to the ground near the spider and the absence of the full light of day seemed a blessing. Corday turned away, as did Sack and others. Only Dana and Young looked long at the body of Trooper Benson.

"Thank God, he didn't live long," Young said.

Dana just looked; silent and grim, he just stared, though once he shuddered down to his boots.

The savages had made a human porcupine of Benson by driving pine needles under the skin. Hundreds of them, a quarter-inch deep before setting them on fire. And there Benson lay, with each needle burned down to and under the red weals on his tortured dead body.

Victorio had kept his promise:

"White men will die the Apache way."

14

PETTICOAT FEUD

BONNIE HAD SEEN yesterday's sundown smokes climbing up from the highest peaks of the Mogollons. She knew, as did everyone in the town of Bacon before sunset, that war had opened above Gutache Mesa. The sounds of guns carried on the wind, and then a courier bound for Fort Bayard raced down from the north.

War was one thing, her curiosity another. All the day before she had put down the urge to visit Beulah Orbon whom she had never seen. Sack's words kept running through her mind—"Go see Beulah Orbon," after he had checked himself while saying, "If you want the truth of it——" Then Dana unwittingly heightened the puzzle with references that had to do with Luke.

The sun had not mounted the eastern range when she got in the saddle and struck out for Queeny. Near Bacon a cloud of silt caught her attention. Horses were moving down from the mesa. The Army, she realized. She rode on, slowly now in order to junction with the troop at Y Fork. The first unit came on, and she learned a little of what her father had left unsaid last evening, that Young and Dana had almost perished in a rear-guard fight.

More than curiousness gripped her as she asked questions. She breathed with relief upon learning that both were very much alive. Then she saw them moving toward her, saw Young staring at her before breaking into a gallop. He reined sharply and sat still in the saddle.

Her first impulse was to ride fast away from him, though the sight of his bandaged face and arms caused her to wait for him.

"You look something awful," she said.

"Are you out here alone?" he asked gruffly. Upon learning that she was riding to Queeny, he told her about Benson and, as she gazed at him horrified, he said, "I reckon you don't know what they'd do to a white woman."

She could imagine, and she did so in silence.

"So if you're set on it, I'll go with you."

Dana intervened with "Don't forget you're still under arrest, scout."

Bonnie saw the flashing of their eyes, the duel between them. She knew Dana's regard for her and she had felt the press of Young's lips.

"I'll vouch for the prisoner," she said.

And when Corday rode up, all smiles and gallantry in clean blue and polished bars, she pretended more than casual interest. Both Young and Dana looked resentful, which pleased her.

Corday had not forgotten yesterday's strong talk by Young. He was quick to place his dislike for him into an order that the prisoner report to him in Bacon by sundown. Raising his arm, he pushed the troop on with one forward sweep.

On the road to Queeny she goaded Young with questions, glances, and remarks. She picked at him in an effort to learn, not only of surface happenings and events, but of all that went on inside him. He answered sullenly, remembering and feeling the sting of their last parting. He was about to ask about her wedding when she said:

"You aren't very popular, Young West. In fact, you go out of your way to make enemies. Just how did you rub Captain Corday the wrong way?"

"I told him off," he replied, not meeting her glance.

"Sure. You'll get around to telling everybody off if you live long enough. Whatever you're trying to do, it seems you're going at it rather aimlessly."

He countered with the question uppermost in his mind: "Are you marrying Luke Mason?"

"Maybe I am and maybe I'm not."

"Why are you going to Queeny?"

"To see Beulah Orbon."

Surprised, he realized that she was examining his mind, page for page, line for line.

"What about?" he asked.

"To learn all I can," she replied evenly.

"If you ram your nose into cactus, you're liable to get stuck."

"That's what I know, mister. But better to get stuck with that than——" She hesitated.

"Say it," he demanded.

"All right—marriage," she said defiantly.

"There's nothing wrong with marriage," he reflected aloud. "Any more than there's anything wrong with whisky. Or six-guns. Or gold. It's people who misuse all of them. Now marriage——"

"So you're a philosopher!" she laughed.

"No. I've been drunk and I've fanned a gun and I've been robbed. But never married."

"You might be hard to tame."

"Like to try it, Bonnie?"

The color crept up under her skin and her eyes were alive with speculation.

"And live on vengeance and powder smoke? No, thanks."

"I reckon I asked for it," he said slowly, his face reddening. "So go ahead and marry Mason. He's able to set you in the finest surrey and drive you down to Silver City and spend a fortune on you. No gingham and sack-cloth for you there."

Her hand fell on his arm. With a look of regret and entreaty on her face, she said, "I'm sorry, Young."

"I'm not," he replied, in stern tones. Nor would he allow himself to be trapped into further conversation during the remainder of the journey.

As he watched her enter the Green Palace Hotel, he was

filled with a strong desire to turn her over his knee and spank her soundly before taking her in his arms. She was a hardheaded, stubborn, independent, spoiled woman.

The door to Beulah Orbon's room opened with Bonnie's second rap. A red-headed woman with a rather pretty face stood looking at her. Bonnie took her in, figure and emerald dress and necklace. She saw freckles, and she searched the pair of blue eyes that now widened a little, either in surprise or recognition, or both, for the real woman before her. She knew that Beulah was similarly engaged.

"You're Bonnie McQueen. Come in."

"How did you know?" Bonnie asked at once.

"Luke told me about you."

Bonnie was thinking she was quick to the point.

She said, taking a seat: "Miss Orbon I'm not a person to fence around a subject. Have you any idea why I'm here?"

"I think I have."

Beulah's unflinching look took Bonnie by surprise. She placed a new estimate on the woman before her and prepared for more than she had expected. A small twinge of jealousy ran through her as she gave due thought to the appeal Beulah might evoke in Luke.

"I'm here for two reasons," Bonnie said. "First, I'd appreciate a true account of all that happened the night our foreman, Charlie Wyatt, was killed. Mr. Sack said I should come to you for the truth."

Beulah told of the mob and the arrival of the Sacaton Kid as well as his leading the militia supported by a miner.

"I'm sorry to tell you," she said, in conclusion, "that Charlie forced the gunplay."

Bonnie considered all this thoughtfully before asking who was back of the deception.

"I don't know—unless——"

"What is Luke to you?" Bonnie asked bluntly.

"You're very direct, Miss McQueen. Luke is all business most of the time. Lives and breathes it."

"I heard that Dan Turrentine named his mine after you." With Beulah's nod of affirmation, Bonnie said: "Luke and Big Dan don't get along. Is it business between them, or is it something else?"

"You mean me, of course." Her expression seemed tense and resentful for a moment. "I could tell you it's none of your business and be within my rights. You know that."

"I do. And I won't think less of you if you want it that way."

"That's the way I want it, all right. But it's better this way. Yes, the main trouble between Dan and Luke is me."

"Well! Do you know Luke and I are supposed to be married real soon?"

"Sunday, I understand."

"Yes. And after that what about Luke and you?"

"I told him it would be all over. But there's really nothing between us, nothing much."

"And what did he say when you told him that?"

"You won't like it."

"But I can take it," Bonnie replied.

"We'll see if you can. He said I wasn't giving him up. And the way he said it—well, I believe him."

Bonnie was shocked. Staring she sat out a packed silence before getting to her feet and saying:

"You don't want Luke married to me, do you?"

"No."

"Then you could be lying just to prevent it."

"Believe what you wish."

Bonnie's glance remained fixed on Beulah for some time. Then she walked to her and grasped her hand. "Thanks, Beulah."

She moved to the door and placed a hand on the knob. Turning, she said:

"If I do marry Luke, you'd better leave these parts." She added, "I mean it."

With that, she flung the door back, and took a step forward. Looking up, she stopped still.

Luke stood in the doorway, smiling, composed, and, she thought, somewhat amused. Across the hall his Indian stood with arms folded.

"You seem surprised to see me, Bonnie," he said.

"I am."

Looking past her, he said, as though to Beulah: "So you two have met at last. I've had this in mind for some time. But business slows good intentions."

"You weren't expecting to find me here, and you know it," Bonnie said.

"I saw you walk up the steps." His glance held up under close scutiny, causing her to wonder if doubt of his total integrity was in order. "Sorry to intrude, Bonnie, but I couldn't wait any longer. I'm riding up to Copper Creek."

Before she could reply, he said: "Beulah, we're expecting you at the wedding tomorrow night."

"I'm afraid there won't be one, Luke," Bonnie said.

His expression underwent little change; only his brows

lifted and his eyes sharpened. His laugh was convincingly innocent.

Bonnie wasn't through. She said, in stern command, "Wait, Luke Mason." She told him all she knew, causing him to look from her to Beulah and back again at her. "Now what have you to say, Luke?"

"That Beulah is my partner on a few good deals. She's a fine, smart woman. Ask your father. He owns the notes on this hotel."

"I'm afraid that answer won't do, Luke. Didn't you tell her you weren't giving her up after you were married?"

"Sure. And I'm not. In her position here, she's the eyes and ears of this town."

"You lied to me about Young West. You'll lie again."

"West? Sure I lied a little," he said, with perfect impunity. "You were a mite too interested in him to suit me."

Bonnie placed his ready answers and composure alongside Beulah's silence and saw either a clever man dominating the other woman or an innocent man wronged.

She placed a last question: "Have you ever kissed her?"

"Often." Luke grinned. "Just like I'm going to do now." He held Beulah's shoulders and pecked her on the mouth. Laughing lightly, he said, "Find out all you can about Turrentine's plans, Beulah."

Next he took Bonnie's arm and said, "I'll see you home before I ride north."

She made no protest. She was too confused.

On the stairway Luke paused and took her hand in his. His face was sober.

"Bonnie," he said, "never doubt me again."

Any sentiment she had felt for Luke was gone. She knew suddenly she would never, could never, marry him.

She said: "I won't ever trust you again. We're through, Luke."

He searched her face for total sincerity, finding it, doubting it. As her glance held strong and her hand was withdrawn from his, he thought her jealous. Only a woman in love was jealous. He smiled.

"You're upset, Bonnie."

"I mean it, Luke," she said, moving away.

He walked on down to the lobby with her, his self-confidence unshaken even when she coldly refused his offer to escort her home.

"You needn't bother. Young West rode up with me. He's waiting."

"He's supposed to be under arrest."

"He is. Captain Corday sent him as my escort with orders to return by sundown."

Luke studied her closely, nodded, and looked secretly pleased.

"Think you're safe with him?" he asked.

"Yes," she replied. "Safe enough."

15

SILVER AND BLOOD

YOUNG SAID LITTLE all the way to Bacon. Bonnie seemed lost in troubled thought out of which she would glance up at him occasionally with intent eyes. What went on in her mind he did not learn, though he burned with unvoiced questions about her meeting with Beulah and the scheduled wedding.

As they rode up to the ranch house she gave him a puzzled look and said:

"What could draw Luke to Copper Canyon with Victorio loose?"

Young couldn't answer that, no even to himself. With curiosity mounting, he was taken by surprise when she said:

"You know I intend marrying Luke tomorrow, Young West. Why don't you do something about it?"

He missed her meaning altogether. Thinking the storm in her eyes and the rising color in her face were inspired by total regard for Luke and concern for his safety, he whirled his horse and struck out at a gallop when it was in her mind that he should take her in his arms. Amazed, she watched him go. Gathering her senses, she walked to the porch and looked at the dust his horse kicked up.

"Crazy man!" she flung after him.

Young splashed through the shallows and raced on north of Bacon. His face was hot with anger, and his lips were drawn into a grim line. He meant to have it out with Luke Mason before the day ended. Copper Creek or Queeny, it was all the same. Mason was guilty of something deep that hadn't entirely surfaced, some high scheme that involved two women, a pair of mines, a murderous Navajo, and the Lord only knew what else.

Stung to the core, he put reason aside for rash thinking. Reason wasn't a good servant now that Bonnie had spoken her sentiments. He felt the loss, the hollow emptiness of his heart. He spurred the animal up the flats, on beyond the Y that forked into Queeny Canyon and the mines, carelessly aware that every movement of his horse carried him deeper into Apache territory. His thoughs unyielding and stern, he rode into and out of thickets of oak, around upthrusts of rock, all ideal spots for ambush, without exercising any sense of caution whatever. Bonnie behind, Luke ahead, he was a detached object moving between them, his mind leaping from one to the other.

The untamed land lifted higher, rougher; rock cliffs spired upward and canyon walls closed off the open world. Colors in the mass of rock formed a prospector's paradise. This land wasn't for the poet or artist just yet. It seemed too merciless for even the grizzled followers of the pick and shovel, many of whom came only to disappear from the face of the earth. As his father had done.

The canyon narrowed into a forbidding dry gut. Oak brush and scrub cedar lined it frugally, and a man wondered why they tried to exist at all. Feeder canyons ran off to nowhere or everywhere, thinning and widening, twisting like tortured snakes.

Young stopped and eased in the saddle. Finding Luke Mason in a canyon that stretched out for miles was next to impossible, and he decided to rim out in order to check the burro road over the divide from Queeny. A half-hour later he managed to zigzag up to the rim. From there he twisted high into the pines and aspens. The view was excellent, and he waited out the better part of two hours before sighting a burro loaded down with pick, shovel, and supplies. A man walked ahead.

The prospector came on slowly until he was directly beneath Young, who peeped out of the brush. He was the old coot who showed his silver rocks at the Frontier Saloon and up in Queeny, Loco Tom.

Far down the slope he saw a horseman. Even in the distance he recognized Indian Joe. He waited and was rewarded at last. Luke Mason came on slowly.

When the ragged country screened him from all three, he moved down in their direction. Pausing where he had last seen them, he hid behind a clump of piñon. They were moving down a twisting trail toward the canyon rim at a slow walk. The Navajo rode ahead; he stopped and Luke stopped. Both were out of the saddle and creeping forward. Soon they mounted again and moved on due east for almost a mile.

Young followed on foot after walking his horse some distance off the trail. He was running at a crouch when the Navajo suddenly fell out of the saddle and pointed below. Luke slowly dismounted.

Young eased to the brink behind a low ridge of rock and cedar. Lying flat, he looked below. There on a wide shelf which hung between the trail level and canyon, the prospector sat cross-legged tapping a piece of honeycombed rock with the poll of a prospect hammer. Next he cut into it with a knife. He crawled along with face close to the ground toward the canyon rim, pausing to dig in, nod his head, and move on.

The whole picture came to life then. Loco Tom was about to lose his life. On his feet with gun in hand, Young paused when Mason broke his silence.

"Hello, Loco Tom. I'll give you five hundred dollars for your find, sight unseen."

The old man whirled and stared up at Luke.

Stroking his beard nervously, he said: "Don't like nuther yer propositiion nor yer altitude, Mr. Mason. 'Sides, how'd ye find me?"

"Trailed you," Mason replied. "You'd better accept my proposition. It's a good one."

"Trailed me, did ye? I gads, I'll give ye one minute to turn and git."

He was moving toward his burro for his rifle as he said it.

He had not taken three steps when an arrow struck him. It drove under his left shoulder blade almost feather deep. He fell forward on his face, uttered a stifled scream, then jerked all over. In another second he lay still.

Young couldn't take his eyes off the old man as four more arrows plunged into the body.

Young remained motionless until Mason and his Navajo rode out of sight over a rise. Still he waited. When he got up, it was to scout them up over the divide.

He returned to the scene and made his way to the body. A scrap of paper in a pockt was addressed to Tom Burton at Bacon. A few silver dollars and some small change and a sheet of paper in another pocket were all Young found. The latter was the beginning of a letter to: "Dear Sister:" It went on:

>*"I have hit at last. Come upon solid float not a month 'fore Apache war broke out. Aimin' to stake my claim come next week————"*

Young examined the large piece of float, tapping it with the point of the prospect hammer. It was solid silver. The surface vein was large and, oxidized by the centuries, looked like iron. Here, he thought, was one of the greatest silver bonanzas of the age.

He looked down at Loco Tom Burton, dead.

Small wonder that Luke Mason was interested in Copper Creek. Then everything seemed to come into the open, like a written page in the sunlight. Mason was clever. He had sent his Indian out on the trail of prospectors; what the old indefatigable dog had found, Mason claimed by the right of force and murder. Then another thought opened Young's eyes wide in discovery.

Mason could benefit by an Indian war. First, Burton's death was due to an Apache arrow. The whole country would believe as much. And beyond this gruesome fact, an Indian war would clear the country of Apaches so he could work this claim as his own without molestation. The trumped-up feud with Turrentine was a hoax.

"There's your Apache war," he said, picking up a piece of silver.

He was not prepared for the next discovery. It struck his brain like blow from a hammer. He sat down, pale and weak, but convinced.

Tom Burton's death was patterned after his own father's! And the murderers were Mason, his Navajo, and A. T. McQueen.

His hand was closing over his gun in a tight grip as though it belonged there. The feeling was good and it was justified. Killing wasn't murder at all. Rather, it was an end of evil. Justice. Vengeance. He humored an overwhelming desire to ride after Mason; until he thought of Bonnie. She told him not to do it. He obeyed, lifting his hand reluctantly from his pistol.

There were better ways of doing it, she said. He wondered.

The sun was hanging directly over the Frontier Saloon in Bacon when a corporal leaped from his horse and cried, "Captain Corday!" In another second he saluted both Corday and Dana and said, spitting dust: "Scouts Denver and Hall report a band of Apaches moving south, sir. Forty horses. Toward Whitewater Canyon."

Troop A and a detachment of thirty-five men of the Eighth Cavalry responded to bugle blasts and "To horse!" A bandoleering of ammunitiion, a great cloud of dust, and guidons split the breeze. Minutes later only dust hung over the ridge southeast of Bacon. Bearded Scout Denver rode abreast of Corday, shouting above the thud of hoofs his opinion that the Apache war party was too large for a decoy.

Corday said nothing, just raced on, cutting through the bend of wagon road and topping a long ridge. Below, a mile off, he saw smoke. Beyond, not a mile south, a larger pillar of smoke lifted black. Out of the unseen distance guns barked.

Troopers streaked down the ridge, hoof-sliding and tearing through brush and beargrass toward the ribbon-like road ahead. The tail men choked on dust, swore, sweated, and damned the Apache to hell and back. Far ahead, Corday broke into a full gallop, holding to the road while the scouts spread out in flanking order to the nearest high points. Scout Hall waved from a knoll and his motions meant that combat lay over the next rise.

Corday split the command, taking the left flank for chase. Dana, with Sergeant Reeder and his tried unit, swung over the rise, turned right and bore down on a burning wagon. Six animals of the twelve-mule team lay with throats slashed. The bodies of the mutilated wagoner and guard were stretched out fifty yards from the wagon.

The Army was late, as usual.

Dana looked up. Corday was running pursuit toward the Mogollons.

The second fire leaped up at Dana's group over the rim of a knoll. A house and barn were still in flames. The Indian postoffice pointed south, and Dana rode in that direction until the trail suddenly played out.

Victorio was deceptive. By booting horses with buckskin, he left no trail as he swung east. The mark of hoofs opened up again a half-mile toward the Mogollons.

"Toward Whitewater Canyon," Reeder said uneasily. "By thunder, this may be a trap."

Thinking the same, Dana called in his scout and talked it over.

Hall said, "It ain't Apache."

"Then this party is a decoy," Dana said.

The scout pulled at his white goatee and looked after Corday.

"The Cap'n will soon know. It looks like big strategy to me."

Somewhat baffled by the deception practiced on him as well as orders from Corday—"You will hold the road clear after investigating the fires, Mr. Dana, until I return"—and fearing the presence of a stronger war party to the east than was reported, he took in the surroundings with squint-wrinkled eyes, and said:

"Mr. Hall, lead us east. If Corday is riding into a trap, we'll be close enough to help him in a hurry."

Reeder's glance shifted from Dana's, though only after he sucked in a knowing grin which Dana couldn't quite fathom. He was thinking the Sergeant might be tickled to see him reprimanded for this slight deviation from orders.

Forty-five minutes by the watch. Dana walked his horses, ordered unbit and graze. He sweated his shirt black, and his eyes were slits under a pulled-down campaign hat as he gazed east, and waited for the brass of the bugle or sounds of gunfire. Only silence.

One hour. Another five minutes. He was halfway between the road and Whitewater Canyon, on the mesa halfway, between obedience and reprimand. Then he heard it, and Reeder and Hall and his men heard it.

Rapid gunfire. Dying down, breaking out again, muffled and weak, short sallies, futile-sounding. Heavy again, now sporadic.

Sweat poured down Dana's face.

Unable to wait there when he was sure Corday's force was in a trap, Dana swung into saddle and shouted the order to move on east at a full gallop. A quarter-hour later, Troop A looked down into the mouth of Whitewater Canyon a couple of miles off.

Dana said what every man of them dreaded, "The battle is inside." Which meant Victorio had carried the fight to his favorite ground inside the canyon where he could pick off the troopers from ambush to his heart's content. And Corday had fallen for it! Then they heard the echoing blast of a distant trumpet. The call for help. It came, long and muted by the hollows and spires of Whitewater Canyon.

Dana cried out and let his arm fall forward. The troop moved up, fast, battle-ready and alert. He led them across the dropping mesa on into the big gullies and up and out of them, obliquely across the mouth of the canyon where they rimmed out single file. It was rush the enemy now. They surprised a big band of Apaches who were taking a toll of Corday's men below. The foe scattered in every direction and Dana was able to drive off the Apaches who were closing the trap inside the canyon.

Five minutes later, there was not a living Apache in sight. But Victorio had won a victory. Seven of Corday's men were dead; ten were wounded. Strategically, Victorio had a greater triumph to his credit, since there was not a soldier between him and the town of Bacon.

The troops junctioned out in the open meadow above the creek, both units rushing the dead and wounded out of the vulnerable canyon. With sentries posted and order restored, couriers raced for Fort Bayard, and every man save the Captain, scouts, and guards worked with the wounded.

Dana had no sooner bandaged a young trooper's arm than Corday called him aside and said: "You arrived mighty quick after the trumpet sounded, Mr. Dana. Were you on the wagon road as I ordered?"

Dana's reply was quick and crisp: "I was not."

Corday's dark look was full upon Dana when a shout from the mesa broke the tension. Denver raced down, crying at the top of his voice, "Victorio's sacking the town!"

In the frozen silence they heard the far-off barking of guns. Like bells, there was a story in the sound: Victorio, renegade, butcher, and general, had foiled and outwitted the 'Frisco Valley Command by strategy heretofore unheard of in Indian warfare. And without the timely intervention of Dana, his victory might have been one of the greatest in Apache history. But that didn't matter now. Victorio was striking at the defenseless town of Bacon.

16

SIEGE

YOUNG WAS RIDING up the last ridge that separated him from a view of Bacon when he heard sounds of rapid gunfire. Before he looked at the town, less than a mile away, he sensed trouble of a big sort. As his glance fell to the body of Loco Tom Burton, he decided to place it in a ravine until he was able to return. Covering the remains and marking the spot in his memory, he struck out for Bacon.

Rifles barked louder and puffs of gun smoke blurred the green of cottonwoods. Then a wall of smoke rose from an outlying house. Horses and riders darted crazily into and out of sight. For a stunned moment Young was unable to believe that Victorio had dared this. But it was happening before his very eyes. The Army! He was asking where the troops were when he saw several Apaches running with burning Army wagons toward the business houses.

Flames licked high from the livery barn and then another house was burning. All defense seemed centered about the Frontier Saloon, now circled by Indian ponies, savages riding, shooting, and yelling, lying to the off-sides of horses. If there was one Apache there were one hundred. And off to himself, on a knoll was Victorio.

He sat erect and still on his white horse watching the destruction he wrought.

Young was riding toward him with pistol in hand when the savages discovered him. Cut off from the town, he headed for the river.

Then he thought of Bonnie. Fear gripped him. An arrow sang by his head and the few devils who chased him were strengthened by another band. It was a race now for McQueen's house, the only cover between the river and the 'Frisco Range.

Suddenly he changed his course. Leading the pack to Bonnie was a fool's idea of safety. He was a little late, however. The main body of pursuers had seen the house and all but two rushed toward it. Young turned back, working in angles, darting first one way, then the other. He was almost in the middle of the enemy as he came into the front yard.

His gun spoke fast. He was lifting it for the pair of charging Apaches when his horse reared high and fell. He rolled to the porch and looked up into the lusting face of a savage. A gun exploded from the door and the Apache hurtled backward. In another moment Young was inside barring the door.

"Thanks," he said, looking at Bonnie.

Her eyes were large and bright, her face flushed. A ringlet fell to her forehead.

"You're welcome."

He fired through a window after reloading his pistol.

"Alone?" he asked.

"Half the boys are out rounding up our horses. The rest went with Father up to Queeny to help protect the town. Sort of ironical, isn't it?"

"Not even an Apache can outguess Victorio."

An arrow flew by her, thudded into the far wall. She raised her rifle, took aim and fired.

"Got him!" Shuddering, she said. "Where is the cavalry, Young?"

A noise at the rear of the house drew Young's attention. Four shots sounded in rapid succession. When he stood by her again, he seemed troubled.

"Bonnie," he said slowly, "we've got to get out of here. They've set the house on fire."

A hopeless sigh escaped her. Going limp all over, she shook her head a moment, then gained control once more.

"No, Young. If it isn't too bad, I'll stand them off while you put it out."

They tried it, but in vain. Arrows and bullets drove Young back each time he ventured outside. The kitchen was burning and the left wing of the house was enveloped in smoke. Flames crackled like hail on the roof. Outside the Indians waited at a safe distance for the smoke to drive the victims out.

"There are several ponies running loose," Young observed. "I'll go out shooting. Cover me, Bonnie."

"I'm not leaving my house." A frantic light of courage or madness flickered across her eyes.

Pretending not to see it, he said:

"You take the pistol. If I don't make it, you know where the last bullet belongs."

Her mouth fell open. She nodded, sending her wide unfocused gaze into the open.

"I won't forget."

He was unbarring the door.

"Young." Something in the tone of her voice arrested him. "Young, I'm going to say it." He waited, staring at her through the smoke haze. "I'm sorry about all the mean things I've said."

Oblivious to the dangers surrounding them, he stood out a thoughtful silence before saying:

"Enough to think about living on vengeance and powder smoke?"

"Maybe," she replied, not taking her eyes off him.

"Maybe you're just excited," he said.

A crashing sound followed. The kitchen roof caved, walls buckled, and the door that closed off the dining hall was blown open. Embers and sparks seemed everywhere. Flames were licking up the walls of the room they were in when Young leaped into the open.

He took in the situation at a glance. The main band of Apaches had ridden toward the river to bring their leader to the kill. Terribio was coming up fast. As Bonnie's rifle picked off one savage, the few close to the house scattered. Young seized the opportunity. He caught a saddled horse the Indians had stolen in Bacon and called Bonnie. She came out coughing and got into the saddle. Young leaped atop a roan.

Knowing it would be suicide to run for the besieged town, and seeing escape cut off in every direction, Young looked quickly for a hole in the closing Apache ring. Only two warriors lay between them and escape to the south. With a word to Bonnie, Young led the charge, gun barking. One Indian slid out of the saddle, dead. The other raised a rifle and fired. The bullet sang by Young's head just as his finger tightened on the trigger. He saw the Apache jerk upward and stiffen. They were out of the ring and racing south before the Indian fell to the ground. They were not free, however. Terribio was after them in full, close pursuit. Bullets, arrows, and hideous yells were real and all too near.

Tingling sensations ran up Young's spine; expectancy tightened the nerves as arrows swished by. Any one bullet or feathered shaft could cut him down and leave Bonnie a victim to their brutalities. He gave her a sidelong glance and tightened his jaw muscles.

A bullet cut through his shirt and stung the skin. A scratch. A ravine lay ahead. If they failed to take it in a leap, it was all over. He said this to Bonnie. They were upon it, their mounts reaching for the other side. Bonnie's horse cleared nicely, though Young's roan pawed at the far caving wall with hind feet for a long second.

Only a few of Terribio's horses tried it. One or two made it, though full pursuit was slowed, and Young and Bonnie ran for the refuge of the 'Frisco River box canyon well ahead of Terribio.

The sun was slipping down over the San Francisco Mountains as they picked their way into the box. The chase had fallen away for the time being. Young concerned himself with Bonnie's comfort and, after climbing to a ledge where a rock curved inward to form a cave-like abode for the night, he went out in search of food. Before dusk he came upon a prospector's cabin. Receiving no answer to his yells, he walked inside and took two blankets, a few strips of burned bacon, cold biscuits, and a jug of wine.

The stars were big that night. They lay on their backs for a long time just looking up into the sky, seeing a thousand and one shapes of things out of the close and distant past. Beauty and sadness and violence and mistakes floated by like burning embers in the panoramas they reviewed in silence. Objects and people they would see no more, a picture on the wall, a dress, a rancher's child and a housewife, sacrifices to flames or arrows, to greed and errors and lack of human understanding.

Then each felt for the hand of the other and found hope and companionship. Though grimy, smoked, their clothes torn and ragged, each seemed beautiful to the other. No word was spoken between them for a long time. A touch, the gentle pressure of a hand, thoughts, and the stars—these were enough.

He felt her shaking, heard a suppressed sob. Reaching for the wine, he held it to her lips. Her eyes were moist and starlit and he leaned close for a long search of them. He drank from the lip of the jug and, feeling her gaze upon him, bent his head to her cheek.

"New houses. New walls," he said.

She looked up into the heavens. "As far away as the stars." Her voice was low and tremulous.

"And new sunrises. And moons. Look over there. The moon gets bigger every night, Bonnie."

She was looking dreamily at the quarter slice of moon reddening down over the San Francisco Range. Her glance shifted suddenly and there was a sharpness in it.

"You don't talk like a man who's all vengeance," she said, her eyes demanding.

"Maybe it's the wine I stole."

"Then drink some more."

Though her command was softly spoken, he detected a stronger light of challenge in her than he had ever seen before. She hinted of quickening interest, seemed to fight it, and he was sure her pulsebeat was racing with his. Warm blood bounded at his temples. She was very near and she was deep and warm and tempting.

"On second thought, maybe you'd better not drink any more," she said.

Afraid his voice might quiver, he offered her the jug in silence. She pushed it away, not breaking the look between them.

"I don't need it," she said.

Her hand lifted to his face. A finger traced a pattern on his cheek. Then she was clinging lightly to his neck, drawing his face down to her. Her lips were softly pliant and sweet, and she was kissing him with an eagerness that said the longing pushing through her veins was equal to his.

Suddenly she pushed him away, and looked up at him.

"I could fall in love with you," she said, a hint of subdued violence almost breaking through her words.

"Why don't you? I'm willing."

"Why don't you make me?"

"There isn't much time, Bonnie. If the Apaches don't get us, you're supposed to marry Luke Mason tomorrow."

She said nothing. Her look lifted to the stars.

She was everything, a symbol of clean pride, courage, spirit, and vigor. She was a fire burning in him, a well of trust and challenge that would never go dry. What was in her eyes and behind them was beyond description. But she was a discerning woman also, and he realized that she was witnessing his struggle with intemperate wishes.

She said: "Maybe I can see new sunrises and new houses now. And a moon. Bigger tomorrow night." She drew the saddle-blanket over her and turned on her side. "Stay close to me, Young."

Before the last red tip of the moon slipped between a saddle of the dark mountains she was asleep.

Young sat near her for long hours. Often he got up and exercised his muscles in order to stay awake. As the night chill fell over the land, he placed his blanket over her.

The stars moved on west, wheeling slowly. Coyotes howled in the distance. He watched and listened, thinking of how she had entered his life. And as he looked ahead, he saw her a part of him. She was altering his plans, holding his hard sense of justice within her own rational bounds. As on the night after the stage robbery, she was riding herd on him, tightening cinch, and spurring him in the other direction.

The dark air of early morning was filled with faint alerting sounds. He forgot them and considered Luke Mason's punishment. But Bonnie was coming between them again.

Love was a queer thing.

Gray dawn was fast approaching when the unmistakable sounds of moving horses claimed his full attention. Tense, he waited, hoping. Then it came on again, and a low babble of voices followed. Apaches. They had picked up the trail from yesterday.

Bonnie sat up listening.

"Quiet, honey," he whispered. "We've got visitors below. They may move on."

Tense and expectant, they waited out the new day. Slow in coming, slower still the untrue dawn masked all nature with gray shapes and visions. And the longer they looked at a given mass, the more it mocked. The world was made up of crawling slate, thick and brutal. Then the sky over the Mogollons seemed to leap up with light. Rock and crevice took on shape. And down below them, not a hundred yards away, where the box widened out to join the open country, were a band of Apaches.

Young mumbled an oath. There was no way of hiding the horses, no path beyond to lead them out of sight.

Looking up at the animals was Terribio. Young clamped his jaws tightly. They were trapped like eagles with broken wings.

Carefully Young drew the rifle to the edge of the shelf and raised his head just enough to take aim. Sharp eyes were on him, and with a hideous yell the band below scattered. He

104

fired just the same, though Terribio was inches beyond the dust kicked up by the bullet.

The siege began. The sun lifted hot and bright. With one cold biscuit between them, no water, just wine, and the clear 'Frisco River rippling on a hundred feet below, thirst and hunger became allies of the Apache.

Shortly after the sun rose over the Mogollons, Terribio assembled his warriors and struck out for their horses. They rode over a ridge and out of sight. Young waited. An hour went by, and part of another when the ruse that failed drew Terribio back. Arrows reached up for them all morning, as did fire from new-issue Army guns.

"I'm cramped to death in this position," Bonnie said at noon.

"But alive," Young said. "Stay down. If they find out there's a woman here it won't work."

"What won't work?"

"I've got an idea. An old scout said it saved his life in the Dragoon Mountains once. Only he wasn't pretending." Crawling to her, he held her hand and said: "But you've got to promise not to move, Bonnie. And don't look. No matter what I do."

He handed his pistol to her. The look on his face was enough.

Flat on her back she watched as he tore his shirt and ripped holes in his trousers. Next he ruffed up his hair and streaked one side of his face with dirt. She flinched, stifling an exclamation, when he opened the flesh of his hand and rubbed blood over his forehead, into his hair and on his clothes.

"Young!" she whispered, staring in horror. "Have you lost your mind?"

"You're catching on," he replied.

She wondered at his sanity when he began to laugh as loud as he could. He kept it up, got to his feet and wobbled toward the edge of the shelf and stood there jerking to and fro, laughing one moment, shaking his fists and cursing the Apaches the next, crying out: "I'm coming down after you devils! Just me and my two hands!"

Beating his chest, laughing shrilly, then hoarsely, shouting defiance, he stood in the open where an arrow or bullet might pick him off at any moment. But none came.

"Cowards!" he shouted. Then he talked in Apache, laughed some more, and stumbled down to the next ledge. There he fell purposely, got up and shouted, "Thought I was done for, didn't you, Terribio?" He laughed for a long time. "But I'm coming down there after you."

He was throwing rocks at the still band of warriors, moving down to them, cursing and shouting at the top of his voice.

Bonnie lay still, listening. Scared and curious, she knew moments when it seemed she could lie there no longer. What he was doing was next to suicide. But what was he up to?

Young was standing and reeling not a dozen yards up over the Apaches. Sucking his own blood and spitting it at them, he moved on down laughing like a madman.

But inside he was scared. Terribio's flat evil face, with its strong bones and eagle-sharp eyes, remained expressionless, still and cruel, as though he were watching some torture he himself had devised. And he might be doing just that, Young decided, might be thinking of new ways of jerking screams out of the strongest white man.

Young kept up the act, stumbling on down to the rock where the enemy stood, knowing deep in his soul and mind that if he failed, his pain would be great and there would be no escape from it. He slid to their level, increasing with small effort his crazy words and antics. He felt the eyes popping out of his head from fear and suspense as he took step after uncertain step toward the towering Terribio. He knew a prodigious urge to turn on his heel and run, just run away from the things Apaches did to whites. He thought of Trooper Benson and slow-burning pine needles under the skin.

It was his last card now, face up to the foe, and he had made the gamble. He must go on up to Terribio. He took the remaining steps, bellowing from down deep in his belly as he leaned close to the enemy.

Facing the bucks, whose faces were sharp and eyes pinpointed, less decisive and more curious, as if the expressionless hate had withdrawn before onrushing dread and fear, Young trembled under the weight of conflicting hope and doubt. His detached mind made insignificant observations: the slick of their oiled black hair and red-leather skins; the gleam of silver and turquoise bands about their arms and the shadows thrown on caverns in big-boned cheeks.

Then he was listening again to the tale of the scout who had escaped a violence by the very act he was now committed to. And he was suddenly aware of the impossibility of such escape. All men were liars, and a man whose job lent him a natural acquaintance with danger could impose on his right and tell a bigger lie which his reputation certified to be the whole truth. His confidence shaken, he groped wildly for some means of defense against the hate in Terribio's eyes. But an act of defense was proof of sanity.

Not six paces separated him from Terribio. His own mutterings and forced slobber and fanatical expression all seemed instinctive, no part of him. He staggered on wondering at his own sanity, wondering what they might do to Bonnie, if they were now reading his every thought. Three paces now, and there was no movement, no sign of attack or retreat among them. They would not run now, and he lifted his hands and uttered an unearthly yell and reached for the throat of Terribio. He had failed, and the realization lent him a fury of a trapped beast.

His act was convincing now that he no longer played a part.

Terribio drew his knife, held it out protectively in front of him, backing a step and another. Young knew he must follow. If they found him sane, he would die. He stalked on, cursing and gesticulating wildly.

"Loco," Terribio said, breaking into a run for his horse. The braves followed at all speed, Young screaming after them.

The trick had worked. What had saved the old scout, who had actually gone temporarily insane in the Dragoon Mountains, had saved Bonnie and himself. The Apache for all his fierceness was governed by beliefs and superstitions that prevented him from injuring a crazy man. What's more, he feared the insane.

Young drew deep breaths of relief. He had acted upon the strength of hearsay to prove that this was so. And he thanked the Lord that it was so.

Bonnie was safe.

17

TERRIBIO'S VICTIM

YOUNG AND BONNIE rode into Bacon an hour later. The town was only half-destroyed, which seemed a miracle in view of Victorio's superiority of yesterday. The Frontier Saloon had been turned into a hospital and its back rooms lodged the town's homeless.

It being Sunday, the itinerant preacher appeared as usual, read his Bible to the wounded, and made himself as useful with bandages as with prayers. He was preaching the big funeral on a hillside when Young and Bonnie dismounted. The soldier and civilian dead awaited burial.

Later they learned that Captain Corday, successful in routing Victorio after a brief skirmish, had received a leg wound serious enough to hold him in camp. This left Dana next in command. Young was pleased.

Leaving Bonnie with the wounded soldiers, who quickly responded to the touch of a pretty woman, Young decided to bring in the body of Tom Burton. He was beyond the cottonwoods when a sentry challenged him: no one was to leave Bacon without permission—Captain Corday's orders.

He was soon awaiting an audience with Corday, who lay in propped position on a cot. Headquarters tent hummed with activity. Couriers came and departed. Lieutenant Botts, nervous, and feeling his impotence, tried to cover up with a pretense of Academy abruptness. Soon he led Young through the open tent flap.

Corday read a paper, pondered over it before saying: "Mr. Botts, write. The courier is waiting. To Lieutenant Dana," he said. *"Under no circumstances will you pursue the enemy toward the Big Dry. General Bent is on the way with strong reinforcements."* He flung Dana's message aside, saying, "That's all."

Young said, "Where is Dana?"

Corday looked up at him then. "Mr. West, I recall issuing explicit orders yesterday. You were to report here by sundown last evening."

"A hell of a time for that kind of talk," Young replied. His calm belied the anger surging through him. "Besides, I've made a report of my whereabouts."

"Which I've read. Surely you don't expect me to believe you escaped Terribio by feigning insanity. Do you?"

"I didn't ask you to, did I?"

"But your attitude asks for measures I've put off up to now, Mr. West. I think it's about time to place you under guard."

"Your face is going to be mighty red when you learn the truth—from General Bent, who'll listen to me."

"Is this a threat?"

"Come to think of it, yes."

"We'll forget that for the moment. But this *truth* you mention, what are you talking about?"

"The body of a prospector named Burton, known as Loco Tom. I saw him killed on his silver vein yesterday up in Copper Creek. I brought the body to within a mile of Bacon where I left him when the Apaches struck."

"What's the connection?" Corday asked.

"The man who killed him laid himself open to a charge of treason among other things. He started this Apache war to cover up his crimes, but mostly to clear the land of savages so he could work his stolen bonanzas."

"Go on," Corday said.

"He's the man whose Navajo rides the pony with an over-size horseshoe—Luke Mason."

Corday sat up, grimaced as his leg moved, and covered his apparent astonishment with "I suppose you can prove this."

"I think I can. I must bring in Burton's body. Plenty of men here and in Queeny can identify him. Then we'll see who files a claim on the vein."

"Granting you're right, Mr. West, how does that prove he started this war?"

"His Navajo's horse left its mark at the Big Dry when Dana's men were arrowed. The mark of a big horseshoe was seen by Lieutenant Botts when the prospectors were killed up at Gutache. Wyatt, who talked up the hanging of One Eagle, was, as any number of men will testify, Mason's tool."

"Possibly." Corday relaxed into his former position. "But I've got a war to fight, not review back to cause."

Young said: "I knew a major once who used his brains at Apache Pass. He wound up with an eagle on his shoulder."

Corday drummed his fingers on the edge of his cot and looked away.

He said at last: "All right, bring in this prospector's body. We'll start from there."

Young rode past the sentry lines with a light detail Corday put at his disposal. Moving north at a slow trot, he knew moments of hope and small exultation. The interest and help of the Army should go a long way in bringing to justice Mason and his cohorts. If McQueen was involved, it was just too bad. Bonnie didn't deserve this, but neither had his own father deserved an arrow in the back. Loving Bonnie as he did, he could never be happy with her if he had to live in doubt of her father's honesty. Better to uncover all and begin all over again with new houses, new walls, and new sunrises.

And Loco Tom's body would serve as a beginning.

Young topped the rise and slowed the horse to a walk. Ahead the ravine showed strong in the late afternoon shadows. He saw a shape, like a body, and spurred up to it. He was out of the saddle, looking down at it. In another moment he was backing away.

Tom Burton's body was not as he had left it. Torn and mutilated beyond any possible recognition, it was a veritable pincushion for Apache arrows.

Young's hopes plummeted. He barely nodded when the

corporal asked if the body should be taken to Bacon. All he could see was Luke Mason's suave face. His ears rang with the mocking laughter of McQueen and Mason. Fate played tricks, and none of them were funny. The war which one or both of these men had set off was serving them beyond their fondest hopes. There were too many hoofprints about, but not a shod horse in the lot. Victorio had done this, not Indian Joe.

The return to camp with nothing of value in the way of evidence wasn't a cheerful task. Try as he did, Young could think of no means by which he could prove the truth. He seemed licked as he entered the tent.

Corday took one look at the body and cried, "Take it away!" His glance lifted to Young when the tent was cleared.

"Mr. West, where's your case?" he said, somewhat vexed.

"It's shot to hell, I reckon." Nor was there much hope in what he said next: "For the time being, at least."

"Sure. Now suppose you come down to earth," Corday said humoringly. "Forget your fairy tales, about scaring off Terribio with an act, that and blaming this war on a man of established character."

Young walked out of the tent. Near the saloon he took in the sunburst spearing the sky from beyond the mountains. Then he was staring at the charred skeleton of a house. From the hospital a long scream pierced the air. The rent healed. In the distance sentries stood still and quiet awaiting the dusk. What they were thinking only they and God knew.

The surge of afterglow was falling back and a growing moon stood strong when approaching hoofbeats were challenged by the shrill voice of a sentry. Soon a half-dozen horses raced up to the saloon. One rider after another slipped out of the saddle until only one man remained.

Young walked to him. "I've wondered where you were. Something new has turned up."

Sack pulled at his mustache. "Heard about you and Terribio, Kid. Nice work. Know why we're here?"

Young didn't.

McQueen was shot about an hour ago."

Young looked up, then away. "McQueen, eh?" Facing Sack, he said it, "Dead?"

"Not yet. We've come for Bonnie. Mason and Beulah and the doc are watchin' over him."

"Who shot him?"

"Terribio. I was with A. T. So were his men. Just this side of the first narrows of the canyon. Seems Bonnie is takin' the brunt of this war. Burnt out, chased out, and now, about the time of night she was supposed to be at her weddin', we bring news like this."

"Is McQueen hurt too bad for me to talk to him?"

"I don't know, Kid. But you ain't none too popular in Queeny. Seems there's been a lot of talk in the last twenty four hours."

"About me?"

"Right. The miners and muleskinners are sayin' you started this war that night the militia strung up One Eagle."

"Smells like Mason."

"Yeah," Sack replied. "But here comes Bonnie."

She walked in a daze. Young thought she wanted to burst into tears but couldn't. He moved to her side and held her by the arm. She looked at him, stopped still and gripped his hands, then turned reluctantly away.

As he helped her into the saddle, she said: "I want you to go along, Young."

Sack intervened. "It ain't the best idea in the world for him to go, Miss Bonnie. Queeny's boilin' mad now that your pa is shot."

"I'm going," Young spoke up quickly.

A trooper said, "The Captain gave strict orders to keep you in camp, Mr. West."

"Tell Captain Corday I'm going," Young replied hotly.

With that, he mounted and rode in silence with Bonnie, Sack, and the cowboys through the listening posts. A cavalry escort held position front and rear all the way to Queeny.

· The large crowd before the Green Palace parted to allow the troopers and McQueen's party entrance. Young felt open hostility by glance and remark. Before he stepped inside the hotel, he knew Mason had sown his seeds in fertile minds. But no word was addressed to him, no attempt made to detain him. His presence was enough, he realized, as did Sack, to put a boil in the pot. But as long as McQueen remained alive, he was safe.

That sort of trouble could wait, he told Sack. What he wanted was a chance to unravel a few puzzles if McQueen was able to talk and scared enough to tell the truth.

Bonnie entered Luke's room, leaving Young and Sack outside. The cowboys waited farther down the hall. Luke was inside, a fact evidenced by the presence of his Indian at the door.

Young motioned Sack out of the Navajo's earshot and said: "It's hard as hell to look at that murderer and do nothing about it."

A little later, Sack knew all about Tom Burton's death,

down to Corday's reaction after the body was brought in.

"That'll tighten the noose about Mason's neck," Sack said. "If and when," he added. "Right now it's your word against his, Kid, with his better'n yours."

He went on: "Here's somethin' else. Them prospectors that got it on Gutache Mesa, Burns and Chalmers—they hadn't filed a claim on the Pueblo strike. But if Mason files on it, we've got him."

"I'm afraid he won't do that now. He's too smart. He'll wait until after this war is over. Unless," he said, "we can trick him into it." Sack showed interest. Young said, in a voice of discovery, "He might do something now if you forced it."

"What the devil you mean, Kid?"

"If you let the word drop, innocently, that I was filing claims on the Pueblo and Copper Creek stuff."

"Yeah," thoughtfully. Then, "Yeah, Kid! By thunder, it's an idea. Only thing, he'll smell a rat if one man is after both bonanzas."

"Then the Burton silver."

The door opened and Luke stepped into the hall. Upon seeing Young and Sack, he moved toward them, masking his surprise with a troubled expression neither felt to be honest. Sack asked about McQueen and learned that he was in a bad way.

"Too bad," Young said. "There's one thing that's been bothering me. I'd like to get it off my chest if he's in real danger." Luke asked what it was. "I accused him of putting my old man out of the way. Is he able to hear me out, Mr. Mason?"

Luke appeared to consider the question seriously before saying, "I'll see about it, West."

As he disappeared into the room, Young said: "God help Bonnie if McQueen dies. Mason will rob her to the last dime."

"What's your game, Kid?" Sack asked.

"I'll tell you later. There's Bonnie."

Bonnie smiled, though she seemed bewildered and beaten. Looking at Young, she said, "Luke says you wish to apologize to Father. Go on in."

Young obeyed. Luke and Beulah and the doctor stepped into the hall without a word when he said he wanted to talk in private. Alone with McQueen, who lay, pale and glassy-eyed, Young sat down by his bed.

"I reckon I owe you an apology, sir, if you're innocent. In your fix you should be honest."

McQueen glared up at him in silence. When Young asked if he had anything to do with his father's death, he said, "No." And what's more I still think Victorio killed him."

"How did you think Luke got the mine?"

"Like a good businessman does. Never questioned it."

"But you didn't look into it after I told you about it. Why didn't you?"

"Didn't like you. Still don't. Trusted Luke. Still do."

"I don't know how bad you're hurt. But——"

Young waited, not taking his eyes off the other. A. T. could be lying. He would soon find out. Slowly, quietly, he told of Burton's murder. The look of shock in McQueen's face seemed genuine. He tried to sit up, though Young wouldn't allow it.

"I hate to do you this way, sir, but it's mighty important. It's Bonnie's future."

He talked on, from the murders of the prospectors up on Gutache Mesa to the death of Dana's troopers. He told about the oversize horseshoe on the Navajo's pony, concluding with Luke's attentions to Beulah.

"So you see, sir, it wouldn't be wise for you to leave things in Luke's hands. Bonnie would be about the unhappiest woman in the world."

"All I've got is just your word for it."

Young asked Sack to come in. Briefly, he repeated all he had said and turned to Sack.

"Tell him whether it's true or not."

Sack said, "I'm afraid it's the truth."

"All right," McQueen managed. "We'll put it up to Luke." Breathing hard, he added: "And he'll make you both liars. Don't stand there! Get Luke—and Indian Joe! Now!"

Before Young reached the door, McQueen went limp. He lay still and quiet.

Sack said, "Better call the doc, Kid."

A. T. McQueen never regained consciousness. He died a little after midnight.

It was a little too much for even a woman born to hide her grief. Bonnie broke and fell to her knees at her father's side. She sobbed until the doctor and Beulah led her away. All was quiet in the room with her going. Cowboys bared their heads and a few shed tears without shame; Sack and Young stood at the door in silence.

Mason lifted his head, drew a long breath, and sent a piercing cold look at Young. His voice was low and ominous as he said:

"What did you do to A. T., West?"

18

A PERSONAL MATTER

TAKEN BY SURPRISE, Young was slow in gathering his wits. Bonnie's grief and loss were scarcely put out of mind before Mason put the question again. As the cowboys stared with growing hostility, Young saw Mason's game: the A-T riders were supposed to carry the question to the mob below. They caught on fast. A pair of them were moving to the door when Young's gun stopped them.

"Stay where you are, boys." Next he looked at Mason. "All I did to Mr. McQueen was tell him what a skunk you are. I did it for Bonnie's sake."

"Skunk?" Mason's brows lifted. "And just what kind am I?"

"We won't mention how you framed me in the militia, how you're trying to turn the same cards on me tonight. That's personal. But what you're trying to do to Bonnie, marry her and still run after another woman, is something else."

"So that's it, eh?" Luke smiled confidently. "I was prepared for almost any accusation from theft to murder."

"That's enough for the present. And I'm leaving this town, leaving you alive. But I'm warning you to treat Bonnie right."

Sack reached for Young's gun, growling, "Hand it over, Kid. Pronto." When Young did so, he said: "Luke, sorry this had to happen here. I'll see the fool safe out of the canyon."

Scowling, he fished a paper out of a pocket and said: "Take it back and file your claim on the Copper Creek stuff. I'm through with you, Kid, plumb through."

"What's at Copper Creek?" Mason asked casually.

"Mean you ain't heard the 'Paches got old Loco Tom?"

Without waiting for any answer from Mason, he shoved the pistol hard into Young's ribs and said, "Outside with you, Kid. Git goin'."

They were no sooner out of earshot than Young said, "You sure inspired Mason to put a rope around my neck with that trick."

"Yeah. Better use the back stairs, Kid."

Sack paused at the rear of the hotel when heavy steps sounded on the front stairs. Luke Mason was wasting little time in taking up the chase. When the town echoed to the sounds of horses moving south, they stepped out into the moonlit canyon and made their way to the horses. Luckily the town was asleep but for a few drifters and drunks. Almost out of the shadows and into the dancing light of a campfire, Young fell flat on the ground, jerking Sack down as he did so.

"Indian Joe!" he whispered, pointing.

The Navajo remained as still as a statue. His gaunt face seemed molded in bronze. He was using that uncanny pair of ears, feeling out with them for the enemy of his master. Sack raised a hand and made talons of his fingers.

Young understood. Indian Joe's work was cut out for him. He would not return to Luke Mason until another arrow had done its work.

After long minutes the Navajo got on his horse and pointed south at a walk. The shadows swallowed him up before Young said: "I'm going to follow that Indian for a while."

Sack asked why and heard:

"I don't know. Maybe just to keep him from stalking me."

He was in the saddle when Sack said:

"I wouldn't be returnin' to Corday if I was you. Won't be safe even there, Kid. Hole up a spell from the 'Paches and whites. I'll keep in touch with you if you'll name the place."

"All right. Say where Whitewater Creek joins the 'Frisco River. About six miles down."

Sack knew the place and Young left him with a last request:

"Watch out for Bonnie."

He moved slowly after Mason's Navajo, on past bright fires and embers with gun in hand. The town fell behind and the going was slower. His horse picked the way out of the canyon where the moonlight was less deceptive. He climbed for the mesa where he could see in all directions. Ahead, south of the ribbon of road at the Y, he saw the Indian's pony jogging along toward Bacon.

Then the ringing of a bell broke the silence of night. Mason was calling up McQueen's Militia.

Young quickly took off to the west of the road. Just when it seemed that Corday's sentries would soon challenge Indian Joe, the Navajo crossed the river, and got off his horse at the ruins of McQueen's house. Curiously he walked around the heaps of charred planks, prodding here and there until he evidently found what he was looking for.

Belly-flat in the shadow of a bush, Young watched him tie a rope to what seemed a square box and hitch onto the saddle. When the horse pulled it clear of the ruins, Young saw a safe. McQueen's, of course.

Indian Joe lit a match and studied a paper. Next he bent to the safe and worked over it for a long time. It opened at last and another light played in his hands. He was removing the contents of the safe when Young decided that the mystery was unfolding like an open book. Here was Luke Mason's first move toward robbing Bonnie. He had not waited for McQueen's body to cool.

Indian Joe had no sooner stuffed the papers in his saddlebag than he hauled the safe back into the rubble. He was off his horse covering the track made by the drag of the safe when Young decided the time had come to act in Bonnie's behalf. Bent low, he ran noiselessly toward the scene and fell flat when the Indian looked around.

Young couldn't shoot. The Navajo's worth in the final showdown was considerable, so he must be spared for that. He waited until Indian Joe was raising a foot to the stirrup. Then he was up and running. Indian Joe turned his head and saw Young, but too late. The butt of Young's gun crashed down before he could move. He crumpled to the ground.

With every piece of paper from McQueen's safe transferred to his own saddlebags, Young took a last look at the Navajo, now coming to, mounted and rode at a fast clip toward the river. Before reaching it, he struck due south in order to avoid the Army camp. He kept going, reaching for the old prospector's shack where he hoped to find provisions.

The moon was falling over the mountains as he neared the San Francisco box canyon. The shack should lie over the next hump. He was thinking of the wine and cold biscuits and Bonnie up on the ledge inside the box when he decided he was not alone. Looking back, he saw a horse just as it moved into the shadows of a knoll.

Indian Joe was the stalker now.

"Come on, Navajo," he said, in a low voice. We'll make a game of it."

The prospector's shack was burned level with the ground, and he rode on warily, stopping at intervals to determine the position of Mason's Indian. He hung on, behind hillock and knoll, emerging at a walk down a ravine, popping up with pointed hat and braided hair around a bend in a dry arroyo; hung on like a leech even in the dark hour between moonset and the first pale light behind the Mogollons.

Young stopped still on the big hump of Whitewater Mesa and looked down on the circular valley where the creek joined the 'Frisco River not a quarter-mile from its lower box. There on the meadow he saw tents. And a trumpeter was sounding the new day.

Lieutenant Dana wasn't waiting for a dawn attack. He stood before the fire amid smells of sizzling bacon and coffee and sounds of horses sloshing in the creek, listening posts spreading out, sentries changing, tents falling ond wagons loading. Aware of it all subconsciously, he was seeing in the fire Bonnie McQueen and he was looking at Captain Corday, and he was also scouting the Indian war party moving south, taking its time, toward the Big Dry.

"Under no circumstances," he growled, under his breath, "will you pursue the enemy toward the Big Dry. General Bent is on the way——"

From over the hill to the south the rattle of the stage drew closer. On it came, its outrider now cutting through to the camp. Soon the stagecoach rolled to a stop with the latest news from the south:

General Bent was having Apache trouble east of Silver City; half his strength was moving toward Mimbres Hot Springs; Colonel Butler, leading a fair-sized fighting force up toward the Gila River, was waiting for Victorio or Hochiti to break out down on the Mangus.

"The hell you say!" Dana exclaimed, looking at the stage drivers. "I'll guarantee Victorio's between here and the Big Dry." Then he said: "Of all the damn mistakes! With Apaches up here, the General looks everywhere else for them."

He stopped short and stared.

Across the fire was Young West, looking at him and saying, "For a healthy breakfast I'll check on Victorio's whereabouts."

"Mr. West, I'm going to break a vow I made and hire as incompetent a scout as I ever knew; simply because I need that information in a hurry."

"Sure. But Corday won't let you move."

"For a prisoner you know a lot."

"Sure do, Dana. McQueen died early this morning. Sack saw Terribio get him."

When they were alone, Young related all that had hap-

117

pened from Loco Tom's death to the rifling of McQueen's safe.

"It all adds up to murder," Dana said. "Which is out of the hands of the military. It's Sack's job."

Young stared lazily into the fire.

"You know as well as I do that Mason's using this war he started, that there's nobody to stop him. Those five arrows in Loco Tom Burton prove that Mason started this war. We need help, military help, Dana. Without it, Mason will rule the mines and Valley with his militia."

Dana turned on him suddenly.

"Why cry on my shoulder? You're free to stop him."

"You're wrong, dead wrong. I can't even shoot his damned Indian until I get more proof than just my word to back up what I've seen. Corday won't listen to me."

"Which means I can't either," Dana replied, with finality.

Young watched Dana closely. He was searching for some means of shaking defeatism out of the Lieutenant. Dana was the last hope, now that Corday would do nothing and General Bent was not marching up here. Then he thought of something. It might work. He said, feigning hopelessness:

"Well, if we're licked, there's nobody to stop Mason from robbing Bonnie. Which he'll do while his militia ties my hands, and Sack's, and the Apaches keep the Army busy."

"Bonnie?" Dana said, with quick interest. Then he looked crestfallen. "Too bad, West. What happens between Bonnie and Mason is of no concern to the Army."

"Naturally, Dana. But to you and me it's a personal matter."

Their glances met and held strong with understanding. Duty to Bonnie stood above all else, all enmity of the past melted into nothing for a brief moment. But Young was suggesting something he had not put into words.

"What are you trying to tell me, West?"

"That Bonnie and Sack and I, and the whole Valley, need *your* help. Somehow, in some way, you've got to find a way of bringing this war to a head, if only to stop Mason. You know the Army, Dana. Maybe you can think of something."

Dana eyed him, said nothing.

Young moved to the spider and ate in silence. After a third cup of coffee, he stuffed food in his saddlebag and rode out of camp without a word.

Somewhat perplexed, Dana watched him go. He was thinking of Corday, who stood between him and any aid to Bonnie. Then he shrugged and tried to dismiss it from his mind. West was asking for a miracle. But the matter wasn't that easily put aside. Because West was right in what he said and left unsaid: Corday didn't know Apaches, and the way he was fighting this war, it could last forever. *West was right.*

He held Troop A close to the junction of the creek and river that morning, sending out small scouting parties in every direction. Toward mid-afternoon he was growing impatient for news, from Young and Corday as well as from Fort Bayard, when a moving wall of dust from up the Bacon road was reported. Hoping Corday had decided to attack instead of waiting for reinforcements, he rode beyond the bend and waited.

It was not Corday, but a dozan armed civilian riders and a stagecoach. Mason was riding south under the protection of a unit from his militia. Halting the stage, Dana warned him of an Apache war party ahead. Mason said it was odd that the Army didn't give chase, adding that he was on his way to General Bent with a demand for troops that would fight instead of letting the savages burn and pillage.

Dana could not check his hot-headed reply:

"While you're there tell the General about your militia that hung Victorio's son. That's what started this war."

Mason smiled, though there was no humor in his face.

"Lieutenant, you may be sure I'll advise the General of your impertinence."

He held Dana's glance for a long moment before ordering the driver on.

The dust from the militia still hung above the south bend when Young rode up from the east, got off his horse, and watched the animal drink from the creek. When he looked up, Dana was approaching.

"Mason was on the stage," Dana said.

"Probably on the way to file on Tom Burton's claim and the Pueblo strike." Under his breath he said, "I hope that's where he's going."

Dana appeared lost in thought before asking what Young had learned from the Apache.

"Victorio's collecting his braves along the Big Dry. Just like you said. Terribio joined him today. White Tail is moving in from the west."

"Hochiti?"

"No sign. He may be there already."

"How many warriors?" Dana was anxious.

Young studied him intently, hoping, wondering, if his appeal of that morning had stirred up something in Dana.

119

He said exploringly, "Is your interest military or personal, Dana?"

Dana bristled, and Young knew that his reply, "Strictly military," was anything but true.

19

MASON'S TRIUMPH

Two DAYS LATER, Fort Bayard was alerted by a running dawn attack up at Pinos Altos, and another between Cook's Peak and Silver City. Victorio appeared to be everywhere at once, but nowhere up about the 'Frisco Valley where he was busy recruiting and arming renegades fat from a diet of reservation food. His strategy held inactive the Army troops Mason demanded and Dana prayed for. Couriers from Dana with intelligence concerning the large concentration of Apaches along the Dry sped from Fort Bayard with replies that any such movements by the enemy were designed to draw United States troops from impending attacks elsewhere. Then, on the third day following McQueen's death, the stagecoach to Las Cruces was burned on the edge of Silver City. The Army was convinced that Victorio was nowhere west of the Mogollons.

Dana sweated and swore. Corday sat out the period of waiting with small alarm at the news his scouts brought in. There was no reason to expect an attack on an already ravaged town, he said. His campfires burned brightly at night and his bugles split the air at all hours.

The stage continued its run through the perfect ambush of the Big Dry road without any attack or sign of Apaches. Luke Mason arrived in Bacon on the night stage four days after his departure. His outriders escorted him into Queeny. One of his men, an A-T puncher, rode ahead and rang the bell atop the Green Palace. The militia turned out fully armed to greet the new king of the Valley. The Silver Bell Saloon was crowded when Mason entered and ordered drinks for the house.

Sack was one of the first to shake Mason's hand and drink with him. He asked questions and soon learned that Luke had "spoken for the citizens of Queeny and Bacon" in a demand for troops. Pretending elation, he plied Luke with drinks. Later he cried, "Speech! Speech!" This pleased Luke, who took his time in telling how he convinced General Bent.

Amid the cheers following this, he said to Sack:

"I thought you'd get smart. Now that you have, maybe you'll prosper." Grinning amiably, he added, "Any objections?"

"Hell, no, Luke? I'm wide open and rarin'."

"Seen my Indian?" Sack hadn't. "Or the Sacaton Kid?"

"He was headed down to file claim on Loco Tom's stuff the last I seen of him."

Luke laughed. "He'll be late for that."

"Meanin' you beat him to it?"

Mason frowned and his eyes chilled over. His hand lifted slowly to Sack's collar; and drawing him close to the dark threat of his face, he said:

"Remember I said you'd prosper. But only if you stay smart, Sack. Understand?"

"Sure. Sure, Luke," came the meek reply. "No harm meant."

"All right." Mason released his grip and said: "One more drink then." He moved to the bar, a little sullen and unsteady, Sack thought, and said: "Drinks. For everybody. Understand? For everybody."

Downing his, and calling for another, he said:

"The militia stays, boys. If the whole damned United States Army moves into our Valley, the militia stays."

His eyes fell like hot pin-points on Dan Turrentine who stood in the door.

"Hello, Dan," he said. "Any objections?"

"Yeah, Luke. If the Army comes, we won't need any militia."

Smiling, Luke asked the crowd for an opinion. Their support was all the triumph he needed. He turned and walked into the hotel and said something to Beulah, who moved up the stairway after him.

Sack waited, saying over and over to himself, "I wish Bonnie and the Kid were here." As he slipped out of the saloon into the street, he saw Bonnie getting off her horse. A pair of men with hammers and saws on their saddles told her they'd meet her at the A-T Ranch next morning.

Sack went to her and whispered:

"Bonnie, Luke's back, and I'm thinkin' he' in talkin' humor." She looked puzzled. He said: "Care to listen in? For evidence, mind you. Go on up to your room. I'll get Big Dan."

"Wait," Bonnie said. "What kind of evidence?"

121

He examined her for an eternity, she thought, before saying:

"I might as well let the cards fall. Luke Mason is suspected of murder and treason."

He felt a little sorry for her as he left her standing there.

The wall between Bonnie's and Beulah's rooms was papered over cracks, affording an ideal listening post. Sack and Big Dan sat on the edge of the iron bed with ears to wall. Bonnie waited.

Luke talked about his trip, asked for a bottle, and resumed where he left off. He would see that the mines stayed open, he vowed, if he had to go all the way to Washington for soldiers. And, he laughed, officers who wouldn't defy him—as the upstart Lieutenant Dana, who, the General said, would be recalled to Fort Bayard at once.

Beulah asked what had come over him; he had changed. Of course he'd changed, he replied impatiently. Hadn't all responsibility fallen to his shoulders; wasn't the town and the Valley looking to him for protection?

"You sounded off big downstairs," she said. "Like you meant to run things. Openly, this time."

"I let everybody know I intend to, girlie."

"Bonnie McQueen taking orders from you, Luke?"

"What are you driving at?" His voice was soft, though edged. When she told him he wasn't married to Bonnie yet, that McQueen had probably left everything to her, and she might have ideas of her own, he said: "I'm the only person alive who has access to A. T.'s papers. She'll jump the way I want it. Else she'll be begging me for money to buy buttons with."

"If she knew you said that, she might not marry you, Luke."

A silence fell between them. Mason broke it, saying:

"Don't get any funny ideas, Beulah. You told her too much to suit me once before. Don't cross me again. Understand?"

"You've drunk a lot, Luke. Sleep it off."

"All right. Help me get these boots off."

"Very well, honey," she replied. A moment of silence, and she said, "Did you file those claims?"

"Naturally. That's why I made the trip." He laughed. "Under the cover of going after troops. Well, I succeeded in both places."

"Then is it necessary for you to marry Bonnie McQueen, Luke?"

122

"Necessary! Of course it is. I can't just up and take everything in a hurry. You know that."

She agreed, reluctantly. Then he was telling her, convincingly, that he wanted all the silver up in Copper Creek for "you and me, Beulah," that it would take time to dig it out.

Sack gripped Big Dan's arm and drew Bonnie closer to the wall. "This may be it," he whispered hopefully. All the excitement attending the end of a chase ran through him as Luke laughed and said Loco Tom was typical of the prospectors who hit it rich in that he never filed a claim.

"Did Burns and Chalmers have a claim on the Pueblo?"

"No. But why are you looking at me that way? I can read you, Beulah. You're thinking I had them murdered in order to claim their strikes."

"And why should I be thinking that?"

"Because that meddling gunman West put ideas like that in a few heads when he accused A. T. of putting his father out of the way for the Queeny."

"You knew West's father, didn't you?"

"I met him once. Tried to buy him out."

"As you did Chalmers? And Loco Tom?"

"Naturally. A. T. wanted to mine up there when the war cleared the Apaches out. Why, Beulah, you look at me like you thought——"

"Did you, Luke?"

He chuckled. "Here are the claims on Pueblo and Copper Creek. Look them over and draw your own conclusions after you learn whose name both claims are filed under."

Moments later, Beulah exclaimed, "Bonnie McQueen!"

Sack wilted. He had not expected anything like this. Luke Mason, apparently running headlong into the trap Young and Sack baited, had outfoxed the foxes by using Bonnie's name instead of his own.

"He beats all for cleverness," Sack said later. "Took the motive right out o' murder. Even if he marries Bonnie, which is his scheme, the law can't prove him guilty."

But Turrentine wasn't listening. He stood there in a daze thinking of Beulah helping Luke remove his boots. Then he turned on his heel and walked off, the most disgusted man in the whole town.

Sack's beaten look as he rode down to a meeting with Young next day reflected his spirits. He was licked and he knew it, tied hand and foot with a positive knowledge that Mason was guilty of murder after murder, of treason that placed on his hands the blood of every white and Indian killed in this war.

He mouthed over and over as he rode down toward Bacon: "It's up to you, Kid. I failed." Telling the Kid that wasn't going to be easy. Not a damned bit easy. He fished out his old pipe and tamped tobacco in it for a long time, thinking, hunting for some idea that might work. But none came, and he jogged on to the motion of saddle, oblivious to everything that went on about him.

Suddenly he came to life. Ahead were two horsemen. Luke Mason and Indian Joe. He stopped still. Mason was shouting. Then he was striking the Navajo across the face with a lariat rope. The Indian sat still until Luke raised both taloned hands and shook them in his face. Indian Joe moved off to the south and Luke continued his easy gait all the way to the A-T Ranch.

As Sack crossed the river, he saw Mason riding south from the ranch.

Bonnie was in a temper when he reached her. "The very idea!" she said. "The very nerve! Luke telling *me* I can't build my house back!"

Looking at the sawyers departing and the sawmill wagon creaking off, Sack said: "Seems he's getting away with it. What's his objection?"

"He's not letting anybody rebuild until this war is over. That he tells me—on my own property! And my own men are afraid of him. Look, *my* lumber from *my* sawmill!" Glaring up at him, she said, "Just what are you good for, Joe Sack?"

"Nothin', I reckon," Sack replied, dropping his glance and swallowing hard.

He turned away before her next outburst:

"I wish to hell I was a man!"

He rode slowly toward Bacon, seeing charred houses, and grave markers not a week old. All pictures of manifest failure. He felt little and unimportant, a symbol of all the defeat about him. The flag above Captain Corday's tent seemed asleep, like the Army up here. He spat in disgust, looked across at the haze of the Mogollons, and decided that any company was preferable to his own.

Dismounting before headquarters tent, he looked south at the dust Mason's horse lifted, wondering what prompted him to strike his Navajo. He thought it might have to do with Young. But there he went, grasping at straws again.

Blowing out his cheeks, he stuck his head in Corday's tent and entered without pausing for an invitation.

Corday was dictating a message. At the mention of Dana's name, Sack was all attention. He sharpened his expression when Corday quoted General Bent, saying: " 'Feeling as I do that our successes in the present campaign do not warrant a contest of issues between First Lieutenant Dana and one of the most influential businessmen in the Territory, Mr. Luke Mason, I am therefore recalling Mr. Dana at your earliest convenience.' "

Sack could not hold his tongue or temper. He said, "The General is mighty damn polite."

"Said facetiously, of course," Corday said, looking up. "But you spoke the truth. If you doubt it, read Mr. Dana's message of the last half-hour. The man's out of his mind."

The message in his hands, Sack turned to the light and read an urgent plea from the hot-headed lieutenant to his captain in the field—a plea for action, in which Corday's forces should move silently at night toward the Big Dry following the afternoon march by Dana, who volunteered to bait a dawn attack; the strategy was to lead Victorio's main body of troops into a withering cross-fire at a spot marked on the map of the serpentine curves.

"Two ridges there as I recollect"—Sack thought aloud. "You could slip up there easy after the moon sets."

Corday smiled his poor opinion of Sack, saying, "A foolish gamble."

"I wouldn't go that far, Cap'n. It ain't so much a gamble as a matter of comparative strategy." He went on: "And, didn't the General say he was recallin' Dana *at your earliest convenience?* That gives you time to try it Dana's way." Pausing for a look at the personal side of it, he added: "Hell, that lad ain't out to hog glory. He just wants a scrap."

For his pains Sack received a brief lecture in military science in which Corday used the word "suicide" five times. No, he would not listen to it. Why should he so much as gamble on a fool's plan of action when the General himself was on the march to the Valley in response to Mason's "logical demands."

Sack perked up. "On the way? When will he get to the Dry?"

"The latest courier reports he'll bivouac on the Gila tonight."

"There's your chance, Cap'n! He could force easy march and be on the Cactus Flat side of the Big Dry hill long before dawn."

Sack departed with gruff rejections ringing in his ears. Winning this war looked almost impossible with men like

125

Dana, who had that Apache know-how, suffering exile while Corday's type of soldier sat on his backbone and did nothing. And the arrival of General Bent would serve only to prolong the war, since Victorio, warned, would slip across the Mogollons to plunder and burn and kill—and laugh at the United States Army.

It had been one more hell of a day. He had started out dreading a meeting with Young West. Now it would be just as big a job to meet the hard pair of eyes in Dana's head. But the thought of standing up to both of them was an ordeal.

Sack mopped the sweat off his face and directed a string of voluble imprecations at the shackles of failure. Only one tiny ray of hope was left. Dim and weak, but somehow it flickered. It was the Kid.

20

BEYOND VENGEANCE

UNAWARE THAT TWO PAIRS OF EYES in the distance watched his descent, Young rode around the last bend toward Dana's camp at top speed. Slipping out of the saddle, he stepped briskly toward Dana.

Sack looked up, a hangdog expression on his face. Dana gazed at nothing with unfocused eyes, sat very still and lifeless with elbows on knees. Bad news was written across their faces like big bold words on a banner.

Young glanced at Sack, who didn't seem to feel that the forbidding silence merited even a shrug, then back to Dana again, and said:

"Hochiti's moving south with about thirty bucks. Not two miles east."

Dana's expression was blank; Sack looked at his scuffed boots. Not a word in reply.

"They're approaching full strength," Young said.

Dana nodded, straightened, and stared at Young, his face darkening by the moment until he seemed ready to release instantly a hard truculence boiling up inside him. As if thinking better of it, he clamped his ruddy jaws tightly and said, "Tell him about Mason's return, Mr. Sack."

Young heard Sack through, learned how Luke had filed the claims in Bonnie's name to outwit them, about Luke striking

Indian Joe, and the order to Bonnie not to rebuild her house.

Dana was on his feet. "West," he said, "I hoped to hell your strategy to save Bonnie would work, but Mason made a fool of you. So did the Mescalero Chief. Twice is enough." He paused, eyes steady on Young. "My first reward for listening to you was Fort Mangus. And you've meddled again——"

He flung a paper at Young, and said, "Read what it got me this time."

The General's decision to recall Dana came as a blow to Young. Mason's triumph. Worse, it was Victorio's. He could appreciate General Bent's viewpoint; he could feel Corday's smug grin of satisfaction; he could pity the Army with its Corday, Botts, and Bent ineptitude at fighting Apaches. But the last line of Corday's order was a further shock, since it drew in Army outposts to his tent door:

Dana was to march his troop up to the Bacon camp before sundown on that very day.

Dropping his hands hopelessly, Young said: "So it's curtains. Oh, well," he added, turning his back on them, "it's all for the best. Victorio would cut this troop to pieces."

Young had not intended dangling a lure before Dana. His surprise was genuine when Dana advanced upon him bristling in defense of the thing that was his life—the Army. He raged on, letting Young know in oath-spiced stabs that one of his trained troopers was worth ten Apaches in combat; that the paramount difficulty in this type of war was that of engaging the enemy; that for two cents he would throw Troop A at Victorio just to prove these things.

"The field is wide open," Young barked back. "And I'll guarantee you won't have any trouble engaging Victorio."

Sack spoke up quickly. "Hell, I forgot to tell you something, Dana. General Bent is moving up, thanks to Mason. Bivouacs on the Gila tonight."

Dana whirled, stared deep into Sack, then far beyond him. Bugles seemed to blow in his head, he was that gripped in thought. Slowly he swept the land and his men and horses, conflict strong in his active face. His voice seemed to fall away to nothing as he said:

"And Corday can't see it!"

Young and Sack exchanged glances.

"It's a chance in a million," Dana said. "Right now we have Victorio spotted. In another day he'll know of General Bent's movements. Then he'll split up and raid and we may never engage his full strength again. Corday and I could bait Victorio and hold him until the General came up to finish it."

Young chuckled. "You're crazy. Corday won't budge, won't let you."

Looking at the sun hanging high and hot in the afternoon sky, he turned to go, paused, and said to Sack:

"I think I know why Mason rope-whipped his Navajo. He let me rob him of all he got from McQueen's safe."

Sack was on his feet. "That explains why Mason headed south. Ten to one they're the papers he was tellin' Beulah about. But one thing is certain. He's out to get you in earnest today, Kid."

"He and his Navajo won't have to look far."

He opened his saddlebag and handed Sack the papers taken from Indian Joe. "Haven't read 'em. You can."

With a final glance that swept Sack and lingered on Dana, he swung lazily into the saddle.

"Take care of Bonnie," he said.

It was almost an order. Dana's hands knotted into hard fists as he watched Young ride off. And Sack realized that whatever stood between them now had in no way taken the edge off their standing feud.

Dana gave the order to break camp. There was yet time to make Corday see things his way. With a glimmer of hope, he led his troop toward Bacon in the mid-afternoon heat. Sack rode at his side, as silent as the mountains in the distance. Dana's marching silence seemed to heighten the tension at the head of the troop. A glance seemed a brittle thing as each examined the exposed mind of the other.

Sack saw Bonnie and the cowboy first.

They came on at full gallop. Dana halted the troop and rode ahead with Sack. Bonnie looked worried. She came to the point at once: something Luke said just before he turned away from her that morning had been lost in her anger, though as the day wore on it loomed up larger and more ominous.

"He said he was tracking down a varmint that was neither bear nor lion, but *bigger game, for keeps.*" Looking from Dana to Sack, she said, "Where is Young?"

Sack looked at Dana. Both appeared reluctant to answer her, thus confirming her fears by their very silence. As a sharpening intensity came into her eyes, Sack grinned and seemed mighty pleased to tell her that Young had outwitted Mason and taken the papers Indian Joe had stolen from her father's safe. This evasion backfired on Sack.

A hint of panic played in her eyes. "So that's why he's

tracking Young! But he——" She broke off, staring up into their faces with an appeal for help.

Dana's face reddened. Fate tied his hands. Sack did his best with an explanation of Dana's recall.

Bonnie said to Dana: "Am I to believe Luke has *you* tied hand and foot, Lieutenant?"

Dana bristled for a moment. "Not any longer, Bonnie."

He was turning away from her, putting his back on the things that chained him, on his long ten years of service, career, aspirations, and all that these things stood for, as precious as they were bloody and battle-scarred; he was shouting it in one brief exultant order to Sergeant Reeder:

Troop A was going down to the Big Dry. Alone! And against orders.

Reeder had a way of knowing what was in the wind.

He simply stood there, mouth open and speechless, a copy of Sack.

Bonnie was suddenly wise to what she had done.

"I'll ride after Young myself," Bonnie said. "Just give me a few troopers, enough to fight off Luke. Captain Corday can't reprimand you for trying to save Young's life."

Dana made himself clear then. "If it was just a matter of West's welfare, Bonnie, I might not do that much. As for Corday, he's blind. But it's bigger than that. Bigger than all that's behind me or all that's ahead for me."

Young rode leisurely between spilling cliffs flanking the road, on up into the open flat and down toward the twisting 'Frisco River again. He knew the river gorged in at the crossing ahead. There Mason and his murdering savage might treat him as they had Loco Tom. The very thought of an arrow driving suddenly through him sent a chill up his spine. He paused to look around.

Only the hot sun falling and shadowing ragged knolls, cliffs, upthrusts of baked rock, dirt slides, and scrub vegetation. All quiet, all still. Not a breeze stirred.

He crossed the river slowly, gun in hand. Every brush screen and rock ledge was scanned closely. The rim held the scrutiny of his sharp eyes. Nothing was seen. Nothing happened. He rode on at a trail gait, more alert and watchful. Then he was thinking of Bonnie and Sack and Dana and Corday, and Bonnie again, relaxing a little, just enough to snap back with sudden alertness.

A bush ahead moved or it didn't; a buzzard circled a cliff; a dry water run ahead hid something under its sharp rim or it didn't. He sweated. Things he couldn't see, but felt, hemmed him in. Luke Mason was in earnest this time. Young asked himself what was in McQueen's papers. It didn't matter. He jogged on. The road was walling in. He left it, climbed up for a look around, a look at nothing but dusty raggedness in the sunlight.

Out of the devil's waste the green of the Valley opened up. The 'Frisco ran south over at his right. Sheer cliffs rose up from the stream to unite the Mormons' ruined meadows and homes with the primitiveness of the San Francisco Range.

His pace held. The sun dropped a notch, then another. Shadows were longer. Now at his right a trail ran toward the high rocks on the far side of the river: the Indian path to the hot springs where Victorio bathed often in the days of peace. He kept going. The 'Frisco River turned off toward the Arizona Territory and out of sight. Sharp curves, and canyons at the edge of the road. A high point ahead junctioned down like a lizard's back to the trail.

Reaching the spot, he reined sharply to his right, swung around a thicket of cedar, and climbed a twisting trail at a walk in order to raise no dust. Well screened from the north by small oak and cedar, he dismounted and sat down.

He saw them ride down the slope of a long thin ridge and move cautiously toward the place where he had left the road. Almost below him he heard Mason tell his Indian to take the left ridge; he would ascend the right slope and go ahead to where they would look down at West from opposite sides of the road.

Young was satisfied; it was just as well that he meet Luke Mason first.

By squezing his horse between two great rocks as Luke moved up, he worked into position where he could surprise him from the rear. He waited, all the while keeping an eye on Indian Joe, who climbed higher with bow in hand and one deadly arrow between his teeth. Being the better horseman, the Navajo outdistanced Mason and soon disappeared under ragged humps. Luke came on up the ridge. The soft snort of his horse was plainly heard. Within a few yards of Young, Mason reined up and drew a pistol, then replaced it and walked his pony toward the summit.

Young let him reach it before sliding through the brush after him. In a low voice, he said:

"If you make a sound, I'll shoot."

Mason froze. Young took his guns and told him to get off his horse and sit still. Mason did as he was told, unhurriedly, apparently at ease. Young could not help admiring the man's sustained poise and self-assurance.

"Well, Mason, there's not much to talk about. We know how you got Loco Tom and Burns and Chalmers; how you got three of Dana's Troop A out of five arrows; how you wanted and got this war."

Mason smiled. "Just who do you think would believe that, West?"

"Why, nobody. I don't intend to tell it," Young said, looking at his gun.

Luke caught on. He tensed and looked for a way out, calmly, thoughtfully, but in all seriousness.

He said, "You gave Wyatt a chance."

"And I'm going to give you a chance—to tell the truth, Mason. What happened to my father?"

"I never met him."

"That's not what you said to Beulah Orbon last night. You told her you tried to buy him out."

Luke showed surprise. A little of his self-assurance fell away; his mouth tightened, and a hint of panic stirred behind his eyes. His urgent look picked up malevolence that burned color into his face. He said, with superb control:

"What the hell is truth, West—a quick way to die?"

"That's for you to figure out."

Thanks. I'll think it over."

"Take your time. Indian Joe will wait. So will I." The sun tipping down to the San Francisco Mountains was no quieter than they.

Then Young fished a sheet of paper from a pocket and said, "Write it if you like, from my father's death on to the end of Loco Tom."

As Luke made no move, Young said: "Pretty horse, Mason. And I like your hat. Shirt too. Now let's change. You wear my clothes for a while."

The sun dropped behind the range before the change was made. Though a lot of the day remained, shapes dimmed fast. Young handed the paper to Mason with an order to write—"or else."

"You won't dare do it," Luke said, putting up defiance ahead of doubt. "Not until you know whether or not I had anything to do with your father's death."

"Get on my horse. You've got a few minutes to think about it before reaching the spot where Indian Joe will take you for me."

Luke stared. Shaking a little as he mounted, he walked Young's pony down to the road, where he stopped as though he had something to say. Then he moved ahead, Young's warning sounding in his ears:

"Why don't you make a break for it, Mason? I won't shoot you. I'll miss you purposely, to make Indian Joe think you're chasing me. You might outrun his arrow."

A minute passed by slowly, and another; the filtered light of sunset fell darker in the walled-off road. Luke's eyes darted from one side of the rim to the other, then back at Young, who was falling farther behind. Then he saw something on the left rim. A shape crouched there. He saw it move, saw the bow lift. Icy fear gripped him, sent hard shudders along his spine. Trembling all over, but still straining his alerted brain for a way out, he sent his voice up to his Navajo even as he said to Young:

"All right. I'll tell all, West."

Young had waited for some show of fear in Mason, had changed clothes and horses with him to produce a dread of death. And Mason, afraid, had by his very words unwittingly warned Young of the nearness of his Navajo. Alerted, Young scanned the rim and saw Indian Joe with bow drawn.

Young, though some distance from the Navajo, fired. Indian Joe fell back; hit or not, he disappeared. And Mason was racing ahead as fast as Young's horse would take him.

Young spurred the animal mercilessly. Mason rounded a bend ahead and took to the brush. He was racing down a hill when Young took aim and fired.

He saw Luke Mason fall out of the saddle, hit the ground with a thud, and roll on down the hill. He was up instantly, clutching his bleeding shoulder, and running hunched over toward a patch of beargrass.

There was plenty of fight left in him. Young was no sooner off his horse than Mason charged, one arm dangling, the other swinging. A blow to the face sent him sprawling face down in the dirt, but he got up and came on again. Young staggered him with an uppercut. Mason lay still a long time. When he came around, he was lying face up.

Young said, "Ready to talk?" Luke wanted to trade. He could make Young rich, he said. "Sorry, Mason, but it's talk —or else—now."

And still he bargained, this time for his freedom. But Young sat still and silent with pistol in hand and long patience on his face. Luke felt the blood flowing from his shoulder and asked if Young was going to let him bleed to death.

"You don't see me stopping it, do you?"

Luke began to talk. Young propped him up and told him to write. He did. It was growing dark when he signed his name to the paper and said:

"For God's sake, stop the blood, West!"

Young wanted to let him die, but he made bandages of his shirt instead. When Mason lay back exhausted, Young sat down, more weary and bewildered than ever before. Though the man who murdered his father was beginning to pay, there was missing the satisfaction he had looked forward to. He had lived for this vengeance, had placed it ahead of everything else. He had time to think now, and for the first time he saw the dead and wounded and homeless, the suffering, all in their true light. And the awakening made him feel cheap.

He got up and tried to shake it off. He couldn't. This was his war the same as it was the settlers' and Dana's. There was no way to avoid it.

And before him sat the man who was wholly responsible for this war. McQueen had been innocent. The urge to kill Luke Mason was strong in him, hard to put down, though it was no longer a personal thing.

He looked at Mason and said: "Get up. We're riding for the Gila to warn General——"

He broke off and listened. Horses moved at a trot on the north road. A lot of them. It could mean only one thing: Dana was marching down to bait Victorio and force the engagement that might end this war.

21

SOLDIERS' HILL

DANA SAW the lone horseman in the road and spurred ahead. Sack followed. A lantern was lit, and for a moment the bandaged rider trussed to saddle appeared to be Young.

Upon recognizing Mason, Sack said, "I'll be damned!" Then he saw the note fastened to Mason's back. He was reading it aloud when Bonnie rode up:

" 'I have Mason's confession. Guard him well. I'm riding for General Bent.' "

Sack chuckled. "So he swapped clothes and horse with you, Mason. On account of your Navajo, eh?"

"I'm not afraid of anything, Mr. Sack. And a man will confess to any pack of lies to save his life."

Bonnie was staring at Luke with contempt in her face when Dana said, "Bonnie, now that you know West is safe, I'm sending you back."

"Where's Luke's Indian?" she asked. Luke laughed, and she said, "I'm still not going back."

"You must, Bonnie," Dana insisted. "An Army man can't take women along."

She said quickly, "Napoleon did."

There were problems that the Manual failed to deal with. Dana thought this was one of them. But he sent her back, despite her voluble protests and threats, despite the fact that he would need the pair of troopers he sent along. With Bonnie's departure, the troop moved ahead into the night, unaware that a silent rider had witnessed the entire incident just out of earshot.

Indian Joe was puzzled. Some dark magic was at work. The voice of the man he hunted had been that of his master back in the dusk. And the man who was his master had fired upon his servant. And he had seen with his own eyes the man they hunted in the lantern light all tied up. The soldier moved on with him. But where was his master?

He sat still in the night, looking at the stars, listening to faint sounds that escaped other men's ears. Trails and night failed to baffle him. He had the eyes of the owl, the ears of a fox. He had orders to kill.

The stars would soon unravel the mystery. His gods were busy. He must wait now, as he had many long years in the past, when the men in Santa Fe gave him up for dead after beating him unmercifully. His gods came to the rescue. They sent his present master who took care of him and taught him later the evils of white men and pointed out the devils who should die. The gods had done this for him. Their price was small. He had no voice after the beating, but he needed none. It was better to listen and serve.

And he served well. Of late his master had said he must place five arrows instead of one, that each arrow was supposed to represent Victorio's resentment for each of the five years he had spent on a reservation. One to kill, four for hate.

A star winked out, and a veil of cloud moved north on the night wind. A coyote howled. The star winked on.

He nudged his horse with a knee and rode south after the soldiers.

The night was nearly gone when he saw them leave their horses and crawl up to the rim of a ridge. This was the road white men called Big Dry. It was hilly and rough and a place where the Apache lay in wait for his enemy during the day. He scouted the canyons and gulches. There was no Apache here. Then the wind brought him smells. Many Apaches to the east. He rode east and saw the warriors slinking through the night to positions where they might swoop down on the soldiers dropping down from the south flats. Men would die.

Satisfied, Indian Joe maneuvered around to the rear of the white warriors. He got off his horse, crawled up a knoll, and peeped down into a small canyon. The horses were picketed to his left. A soldier stood guard. Another sat on the ground to his right. The light was not good. His eyes closed and opened slowly. Now he was the owl. Several men became men instead of rocks and still shapes. One of them wore the clothes of the man his master said he must kill.

He watched the man for a long time, until the sky behind the big horn of the canyon paled with a hint of dawn. He was thinking: his master had not ridden north; therefore, he had gone south; and he was not here; thus he must be farther south. He should ride after his master. But first——

He slipped down the knoll to his horse and returned noiselessly. In his hands were a bow and five arrows.

General Bent met Young with a hard glance and a question:

"What's important enough to break into a man's sound sleep at this time of night?"

Young looked into the eyes of the short, iron-faced man and replied:

"Victorio has his full strength up on the Dry."

"Corday send you, West?"

"No, sir. Just my regard for you and a desire to see this war end."

The General frowned, looked at the walls of his tent, and said:

"Is Lieutenant Dana back of this?"

"No, sir. Look, General, I'm not an Army man. But I know the Apache. This is your one big opportunity to engage the enemy. If you wait until tomorrow, he'll scatter and keep you jumping for months to come. You could surprise hell out of them if dawn found you well stationed up there."

Bent laughed. "Strategy, West, is the——"

"I know. But Victorio never went to the Military Academy." Seeing the red creep up in the General's face, Young said, with intent to goad him on, "But he knows how to draw officers like Botts and Corday into chase and slaughter."

"Mr. West, are you aware whom you're talking to?"

"Sure. The man who can win this war—if he's not afraid of the politicians in the Indian Ring." The General was up, glowering, but Young kept on: "If he's not too Ute and Arapaho minded to think Apache in Apache country."

"I wish you were an officer under me, West. I'd break you in a hurry."

"I don't doubt that. Any general who would recall a man like Dana, the only officer in the 'Frisco Valley who knows how to deal with Apaches, is likely to fire any man. Incidentally, Mason had you do it. Read this."

The General couldn't believe the confession he read. But he had to believe it. And he learned then how this war had started, how Corday had been wrong and Dana right.

"How did you get this, West?" he said at last.

"Shot and beat it out of him." A spark of admiration replaced the anger and confusion in the General' face. Young did nothing to lessen it as he said: "But finding my father's murderer isn't enough, sir. That's why I'm here."

General Bent walked to Young and held out his hand.

Young rode far ahead of Bent's moving columns. He was thinking of the General's last show of astonishment when he advised him of Dana's march toward the Big Dry in the night. Bugles blasted forth and troops came to life shortly after that.

The dawn wasn't too far off, and Bent's troops were too far behind. The light in the east wasn't visible yet, though soon a pale push would outline that rim of the world. From lead and pewter colors to what? The color of blood?

His horse was tiring, and he knew a horse liked sleep in the wee hours, but he spurred him on. Dana needed what he could give him, a promise that the general was on the way. He was cheering Dana on, thinking of Bonnie and all she meant to him, looking at Mason as the verdict sounded, wondering where Sack would go next when the dawn gave its first warning. The Big Dry wasn't too far off; but farther than the dawn.

Shadows took on shape and dimension in the mock light. Nothing was true that didn't move. It passed and the morning came on. Then he heard it, dimly to the south, gunfire.

The dawn attack.

Something moved ahead. It came on. A horse and rider. Young slowed, took to the side of the road, and skirted east. But the rider did the same. They were nearing each other when recognition came.

The rider was Indian Joe.

The Indian reined up sharply, stopped, and stared. In another second he whirled his horse and struck out across the flat toward the hills.

"Thought I was Luke," Young said, racing after him. Unless he overtook the Navajo, he might never again see the instrument of death that struck down his father and others. The Indian was big and strong and cunning. He ran south, and doubled back north, and seemed content to hold that course, as though the scene of battle would give him protection.

Indian Joe's horse was the fresher of the two. He was out of sight, gone, when Young reached a spot on the flat where the smoke of battle lifted white in the distance.

From far up the north road, above the bark of rifles and Apache throat yells, a trumpet sounded. Young wondered. It didn't make sense, not until the answer came from down in the Big Dry. Now Young knew the bugle blast from the north was Corday's.

His spurs dug into the tired animal's flanks. A leap forward and the motion slowed. Sweat lathered and there was foam at the bit. But the pony was game and the drop down off Cactus Flat was just ahead.

Minutes later, Young looked down on the battle. Ponies of Victorio, Terribio, Hochiti, and White Tail charged up and fell back, in waves; and Dana's valiant troop held the ridge. But the odds! He couldn't survive long unless help came.

An arrow struck Young's horse in the neck. The animal screamed and bucked for a moment, then went down. As Young hit dirt on his back, he saw Indian Joe in the road fitting another arrow. He shot from the hip and the Navajo whirled completely around, then came on running with knife drawn.

The pistol left Young's hand as he stumbled and rolled down a long slope. Indian Joe leaped after him, slashing out as he landed on his feet with the agility of a cat. Young kicked at him, missed, and the Navajo fell atop him. Twice the blade seared the flesh of Young's shoulder and chest before his hands gripped Indian Joe's knife arm at the wrist. But only for a second. The other was free and reaching for his throat. With a mighty heave Young threw him off and spun on his back. Indian Joe was near a drop when his feet started a small slide. He fell forward and clawed at the earth. Young made a dive for the knife, knocking it over the ledge. But in doing so he was caught in the slide.

They tumbled head over heels, hanging on one to the other, breaking, rolling through sharp rocks and yucca daggers on down to the last steep drop. Both were dazed, cut, and bleeding when they sat up in the dry, rocky creek bed, half-buried in silt and rocks.

The Navajo staggered to his feet. Blood streamed out of

137

his side where Young's bullet entered. Oblivious to pain or blood, unarmed, Indian Joe stood on his wobbly legs and glared as his hand formed the talon of death. With one brutal aim in mind, his eyes glazing over, he took the steps separating them.

Young tried to crawl away, though his muscles failed to respond. He fell forward, his face half-buried in the dirt, and lay still.

Indian Joe's last effort saved Young's life. He turned Young face up, fastened a hand at his throat, then jerked spasmodically and died.

Young heard nothing for a long time. The first sound came out of limitless space in which he just drifted. Bugles played in the distance softly, strangely. Then they sounded harsh and real and guns barked closer and louder. Yells rang in his ears and the acrid smoke of battle burned his nostrils. He raised his head. Indian Joe lay beside him, eyes open and dusty and determined even in death.

He managed to sit up. The battle raged on directly above, below, and on the ridge Dana held. He got to his feet and stumbled toward the ridge, holding himself up by sheer force of will. An arrow sang past him. A bleeding savage climbed up a few feet with knife drawn, then slid back and died. Over toward the canyon, Victorio came on with another wave of shouting riders. Directly ahead, Hochiti led a column of braves. The Apache was concentrating his attack. Victorio wanted the ridge Dana clung to stubbornly.

Suddenly Young realized that no aid had reached Dana. He had no memory of time. He might have been unconscious seconds or hours. But he was awake and alert now. Dana's troop was fighting the devils front and rear, holding on in a futile death stand.

Somehow he reached the base of the ridge and lay still under an oak bush. Victorio was tearing up the eastern slope. Terribio charged the opposite side.

He was crawling up the side, hugging a V washed in the slope when a trooper rolled down toward him, dead before a yucca trunk stopped his motion. A rifle slid on down. Young caught it, then moved on up for the soldier's pistol. The roof of the ridge was close now. His head popped above it. A thirty-foot flat here, it twisted north by east with every width from nothing to a half-hundred feet. Dana was down the line. Sergeant Reeder, blood on his face and hat, was pointing a pistol in Young's face.

"Hold it, Reeder!" Young cried.

Nodding, Reeder spat lustily, then fired down the hill.

"Better work the west side," he said. "Terribio made the top twice. Will do it again."

Young moved on, firing as he ran. He fell beside a trooper and took aim.

Sack slid into position alongside him and said: "Glad you got here, Kid. See the General?"

"On his way," Young said.

"Slow, ain't he? He fired, lay flat, and peeped up.

Young stiffened. The grating file of a bugle tore across the morning. Out of the north. Was Corday leading his unit on crutches? There was no time for any answer, Terribio's horde was reaching up with horses and war shrieks, a split force angling up toward center, greased bodies lying to the off-sides of ponies.

"Hold for cross-fire!" Dana yelled, and Sergeant Reeder picked it up.

War paint and yells and the thunder of hoofs and the screen of dust rushed toward the knolltop. Red flannel head-bands above fanatical eyes, dead troopers' pistols and rifles, bows drawn, a knife up, horses eyes wide and rolling, all these rode up to the crest, to the order of "Fire!" Rifles and pistols spat down with livid fury, like a cutting scythe. The morning seemed ripped apart. Horses screamed and savages leaped high in bloody agony. The forward wall rolled back on Terribio's main body; death and the thrashing of death blunted the point of his spearhead, though the angling edges, disorganized, bunched and scattered, charged up and over the top.

A dozen braves fought among the troopers, firing, hacking, screeching. They fell and some of Dana's precious few went down with them.

Dana was bleeding, but listening. No trumpet sounded.

22

THE LAST POST

BELOW, TERRIBIO RE-FORMED for another charge, while on the opposite side Victorio and Hochiti junctioned for an upward sweep.

Sack, hatless, ear nicked and dripping red, looked at Dana. And Young was doing the same, reloading, and wondering about many things, looking north and south, and listening, and stabbing Dana again with curious glances.

This was First Lieutenant Dana's choice. It was also his last battle, regardless of valor or victory. Young felt pity for him, and resentment at Regulations that put disobedience ahead of guts. Then he was waiting, looking down the barrel of his rifle, squinting against the early sunlight, for the order to fire. It sounded and the Apache wave caught it, broke, fell, re-formed suddenly, and drove all the way to the top in numbers.

Bugles! From the south. Cavalry spilled down off Cactus Flat, guidons splitting the breeze, troopers yelling. General Bent!

Victorio heard and saw. He was nearing the top of the ridge when he paused. A yell issued from his throat. Some of his warriors heard, others didn't. But the blast of the trumpet scratched into the ears of all. Hate held them for another stab, and the flesh of oiled men touched the flesh of men in blue, blood to blood and death to death. Men writhed and stared at the last picture of life they would ever see; others touched the arrows in sides and bellies with disbelief.

Then the hill recovered. Dana still held it. By the voice of a trumpet he held it.

Hochiti and White Tail lay dead within a yard of each other. Terribio stood at the foot of the hill. Young's face bled at the cheekbone. He sprawled on his belly and sucked in air. Sack sat cross-legged, dazed, mouth open, with half his red mustache singed. And Dana——

He bent over Sergeant Reeder, his face as grim as death. Reeder lay with an arrow slanting up under his ribs.

He said: "I'm hard to kill, Lieutenant. But this is it. Wish to hell I had time to tell the General that Corday's dispatch never reached you, that——"

Dana's hand closed over Reeder's. The tough sergeant was gone.

Dana seemed unaware of the running battle toward Big Dry Canyon, of the closer slaughter of Victorio's braves down in the draw, of Corday's spread off to the northeast, where savages on foot tried to outrun cavalry horses. He was looking up at the sky, then all about him, into the faces of the living and the dead. His hands worked into and out of fists, his jaw muscles ridging and crawling.

His eyes fell to the band of Apaches surrounding Terribio at the base of the ridge. He saw them raise rifles and string bows. He smiled. There was no retreat in them. Arrows showered up at him. A bullet cut through the campaign hat.

140

"Belly-flat!" Young shouted.

Dana stared at him, still holding the crisp, thin smile on his face. It wasn't in his eyes.

"For once you were right, West. Victorio was here. Why don't you tell me you were right?"

Young had no answer.

Terribio's horses were circling. Up they came. A dozen braves, Terribio in the lead, his torn face red and pulpy. Straight ahead, no deploying of his remnant band, no strategy in mind, nothing but hate and desire to kill. Rifles barked and three of his horses went down. Oblivious to any loss, he came on, his glance fixed on one man.

It was Young.

As Young stared into the cold, savage face he saw purpose; however insane his charge, there was no denying the lust for vengeance in Terribio's eyes. Then suddenly Young knew why. Terribio had recognized the man who duped him by playing crazy.

He was halfway up the hill when Dana lifted his pistols and walked down to meet him. No yell of protest from above seemed to reach his ears; no savage cry slowed his step. He walked on, firing, paying no attention to bullets or arrows, strode on like a god immune to mortal weapons. And nothing seemed to touch him. He was battle-mad, and drunk on the picture of carnage, but he was something to see and remember as he advanced on Terribio.

Young was moving after him, yelling at the top of his voice, "Get back, Dana! It's me he wants!" But Dana had no ears for him; he kept going and Young followed.

Even the wounded on the ridge reached for guns and blazed a path for their Lieutenant. The dozen Apaches who moved up were cut down to three, two, one. Terribio fell and Dana walked on toward him, firing.

There was nothing left for him to fight. He stood still for a long moment, alone, looking up from the dead into the western sky. Then he turned around and slumped forward on his face.

They brought him up gently and placed him on his back. He was still alive, but he was no god—three bullets had entered his body.

Captain Corday's wounded leg burned with pain. And he was saddle-soft. But these discomforts were of the body. What he felt had begun with annoyance last evening when Dana failed to appear as ordered. After that things went from bad to worse. Dana's disobedience became an established fact. Next Bonnie McQueen rode in flushed of face and demanding. She admitted Dana's march and she shook Corday up inside when she told of Mason trussed to saddle with a note from West on his back—he still couldn't believe that Mason had confessed to murder and crimes tantamount to treason, as Bonnie said. Angry, confused, and boiling mad at Dana at whom he meant to throw the book, he flatly refused to go to Dana's aid. He would never forget the picture of Bonnie McQueen—she was imperious and courageous and decisive all at once. A woman of temper, she grasped at a straw and flung it in his face:

He knew where he could go with her compliments. As for herself, she would round up every man in Queeny and ride to Dana. She would use McQueen's Militia "to protect his Army!"

He watched her go, and he felt foolish, and he heard in tomorrow's echo the laughter and scorn she was bringing down on him. And when she returned with a small civilian army, he reluctantly ordered his entire strength to the Big Dry. The ride was long and hard; with every jarring impact of hoof against ground, he resolved to push the case against Dana to a just end, the disgrace he deserved.

And now—in the morning sunlight, with victory over the Apache Nation assured, he saw no reason to change his mind about the hot-headed Lieutenant; in fact, the very temerity of the man was, militarily, suicidal. Yes, he would throw the Articles of War at Goodell Dana, fool of Fort Mangus.

His chance was drawing near. The dead and wounded were separated in the wide, dry creek basin. General Bent's tent was up and the flag waved in the breeze. Bugles sounded. Surgeons and doctors worked. Ambulance wagons rolled down the hill. A cavalry unit herded prisoners toward the picket line. Sporadic firing rolled across the knolls to the east. The battle was over. It was a victory for civilization.

McQueen's Militia bunched, and a woman, Bonnie, rode at the head. Corday winced, thought of how the militia had fought, and laid his annoyance to Dana. And where the devil was Dana?

As he rode toward the General's tent, he saw Young West standing with head bared alongside his equal in audacity, Sack. And Bonnie was off her horse and kneeling to the ground. General Bent stood still and quiet, looking down at her. Then a captain stepped before General Bent and saluted.

"Regret to report, sir, Victorio and ten of his band got away."

"Too bad, Captain," Bent replied. "All the other Apache leaders are dead."

Then he asked about Luke Mason.

"Somebody put five arrows in Mason before dawn," Sack said. Bent glanced at West, who looked wise and said he wasn't guilty. The General asked a lot of questions about the origin of this battle and the sudden plan of strategy before he glanced up at Corday.

Only then did Corday see Dana on the ground with his head in Bonnie's lap. Their eyes met and there was nothing friendly in the glance between them.

"Captain Corday," General Bent said, in a stern voice, "did you order Lieutenant Dana to the Big Dry after receiving my orders for his recall?"

Corday stiffened to attention and looked at the little martinet. But Bonnie's big green eyes were stronger. They pulled at his. He tried to avoid her and his glance fell on West. There was fire and threat in the face of the man he could no longer call prisoner. Bonnie smiled up at him and spoke in the voice she had used in Las Cruces at the dance:

"The General asked a question, Captain."

Corday cleared his throat. "I ordered him to the Big Dry, sir."

Bonnie got up and went to Corday. Before the General and the soldiers and McQueen's Militia she kissed the Captain full on the mouth.

Dana's eyes were closing when she reached him. "Good girl, Bonnie," he said, reaching for her hand. "Where's that worthless scout—West?"

"Right here," Bonnie said.

"Take care of her, West. Orders! From the General of Fort Mangus."

His voice fell to a whisper. He clung on a moment, to speak his last words:

"It's here, Lieutenant Dana. This is the last post."

He settled down and lay still.

A long silence fell over the scene of battle. It was eloquent and alive and memorable with all the things men lived and fought and died for; with the conflict inside men, and opinions of right and wrong as written into inviolate Articles of War and life itself; with one life and one man's fault and virtue—temper and valor—burning across battlefields and memories in the final shape of greatness.

The General looked up into the sky, reverently, prayerfully. Corday tensed with feeling. Sack swallowed hard and tamped tobacco in his pipe. Young stared out over the sunlit knolls through misted eyes until Bonnie broke the spell.

"Young, you heard what he said, didn't you? Well, you'd better do something about it, 'cause I'm fixing to cry."

She was in his arms, her hands clinging to his neck, her face warm and wet with tears. Young held her close to him, roughly at first, then gently. They were one now. One for always.

THE END

www.ingramcontent.com/pod-product-compliance
Lightning Source LLC
Chambersburg PA
CBHW020139180626
46810CB00004B/1642